SHE'S SO BAD

SHE'S SO BAD

BONITA FABIAN

SHE'S SO BAD

Send publishing enquiries to bonniefabian@gmail.com.

This is a work of fiction. Names, characters, places and incidents either are products of the author's imagination or are used fictitiously. Any resemblance to actual events or locales or persons, living or dead, is entirely coincidental.

Publishing Consultant: AuthorPreneur Publishing Inc.—
authorpreneurbooks.com
Editor: Laura Ellen Joyce
Interior Designer: Amit Dey—amitdey2528@gmail.com
Cover Designer: Zizi Iryaspraha Subiyarta

ISBN 979-8-9891674-3-2 (paperback)
ISBN 979-8-9891674-4-9 (ebook)
ISBN 979-8-9891674-5-6 (audiobook)

FIC025000 FICTION / Psychological
FIC031080 FICTION / Thrillers / Psychological
FIC030000 FICTION / Thrillers / Suspense

Contents

Chapter One

Welcome to Sardinia

Caroline and her stepdaughter Julia heard a squeal, then a crunch as the taxi reversed. They sensed an ominous bump in the road as the taxi lurched backwards. The two women hurriedly exited the car, and they saw, to their horror, a blood-splattered bundle of fur on the cobbled driveway. As they bent to inspect the remnants of the cat, the driver hurled their suitcases out of the trunk. Without a word, he sped away. If the ride from the train station had not been prepaid, he would not have received any money from them.

"Fermatti. Stop! Stop!" Caroline shouted after the driver. Her voice was drowned out by the ringing of the early morning church bells.

Aunt Rosalia came bounding down the worn steps, her eyes wide with horror. "Chicco." The word stuck in her throat. "My baby. Oh my god." She bent down and scooped the lifeless body up into her arms. "How did this happen?" she cried.

"Aunt, I'm so sorry. The taxi driver didn't see him," Caroline explained. "He drove over him and raced away."

Rosalia clutched the lifeless body against her chest, leaving bloody splotches on her white apron.

"Salvatore!" Rosalia called out to her husband.

Salvatore came down the front steps, barefoot. "What happened to Chicco?" His eyes darted from the splatter on the ground to the bundle in his wife's arms. He ripped off his T-shirt and wrapped it around the clump of fur then gingerly removed the cat from Rosalia's clasp.

Rosalia took out a crumpled handkerchief from the pocket of her apron and dabbed her eyes. "Salvatore, take Chicco and bury him in the back garden. Under the oak tree." She blew her nose. "He was such a good boy. He didn't deserve such a bad ending."

Salvatore was too distressed to greet his guests, and they were too distressed to notice this lapse.

Rosalia looked up at the two women. "This is not the welcome we were all looking forward to," she said, "but Chicco is dead and there is nothing we can do."

"The driver was heartless – he didn't even care," said Caroline. She picked up the two suitcases and set them upright on their wheels.

"I guess he is used to roadkill," said Julia. "It's probably like murder. They say that after the first one the rest are easy."

Caroline shot her stepdaughter a look of disbelief. *They hadn't been there for five minutes, and she had already said something inappropriate.*

Rosalia ushered the women up the steps into the house. It was a large two-story stucco structure with a sloping terracotta roof. The smell of freshly baked bread came from the kitchen, and Rosalia led them there. A large wooden table was set for breakfast. On a flat wooden board, a round, crusty loaf of artisanal bread was ready to be sliced. A selection of cheeses and jams were set out to one side. Rosalia removed the Moka pot from the stove and poured coffee into their mugs. Salvatore joined them in the kitchen. He was a big man who habitually stooped beneath the door frame to avoid hitting his head. He stopped at the kitchen sink, soaped his arms and hands, and scrubbed them vigorously under hot water to remove every scrap of the dead animal.

"Now I can greet our honored guests in the right manner," he said. He put out his hand and shook each of theirs. "Caroline, you get younger every time I see you," he said. Then he turned towards Julia. "At last, I get to meet you," he said. "I am sorry about the loss of your father."

Rosalia held her hand against her chest and looked at her husband with sad eyes. "You buried Chicco?" she said. "Do you think he will be comfortable?"

"Yes. I laid him on a bed of straw in the ground, under his favorite tree. If there is a cat heaven, I am sure he will be there."

When Salvatore smiled, his whole face lit up. From the moment Caroline had met her aunt's new husband, she had liked him. She was happy that her aunt had found love again after being a widow for so many years.

Caroline suddenly felt very tired from the jetlag. The journey from Miami to Sardinia was long and arduous, with stops and starts along the way. Julia, much younger at thirty-five, was able to bounce back from sleep deprivation much quicker.

As if Rosalia read her thoughts she said, "I'm sure the two of you are exhausted. Let me show you to your rooms so that you can freshen up and rest."

Caroline was pleased that she could understand her aunt's Italian. She had moved to America as a child with her parents but her frequent trips to Sardinia to visit the family kept the language alive for her.

As they left the kitchen, Rosalia turned to Caroline. She took her arm and gently rubbed it. "You have been through such a lot since Stuart died," she said with furrowed brows. "It must have been a great shock to you both."

"It was a terrible shock," Caroline said. "I hope that being here in Sardinia with you all will give us some time to heal. I brought Julia with me to give her the space to grieve too."

Julia pursed her lips. She raked her manicured nails through her hair to sweep it out of her eyes. "To be honest, Caroline," she said, firmly, "I came here more for your sake than for mine. This is your family so it's meaningful to you."

She bit the corner of her lips. "Quite frankly, leaving my husband behind, because he has to work, makes this harder on me."

Caroline kept quiet, she wanted to remind her stepdaughter that she had not forced her to come on the trip, but it wasn't worth an argument.

Rosalia led the women down the hall and stopped at the open door. "Julia, this is your room. It's next to mine."

The bed was made up with crisp white cotton sheets covered with a large white, fluffy duvet. A vase of sunflowers stood on the side table.

"Where is the bathroom?" asked Julia, flicking her long blonde hair from side to side while studying herself in the full-length mirror.

"You will be sharing our bathroom," said Rosalia. "It's down the hall across from our bedroom."

Julia's eyes widened. "There is no en-suite? I can't share a bathroom," she said. "That's not happening."

"Sweetie," Caroline said, "in Europe things are different."

"Where is Caroline sleeping?" Julia asked Rosalia.

"Upstairs. We have a small separate apartment."

"Does it have a bathroom?"

"Yes, with a shower. I thought it would be nice for your mother. There is a little kitchenette. It's more private."

Julia turned to Caroline. "I'm sure you won't mind," she said, "if I have that apartment instead?"

"That's fine with me," Caroline answered. "I am just happy to be here. Any room is perfect. We are fortunate that Rosalia and Salvatore have kindly allowed us to stay with them."

"Okay, that's settled then," said Julia. She lifted her suitcase and carried it up the stairs to the little apartment.

"I wanted you to have that," Rosalia protested, "but whatever…"

"It's okay," Caroline said. "Julia has had a rough time with her father's death."

"It must be very difficult for both of you. What did he pass from?" asked Rosalia.

"A heart attack. It was very sudden."

"Had he been sick?"

"No. He was healthy, a little overweight, and of course overworked. I think the stress killed him," Caroline said, tearing up.

"I know you loved him very much," Rosalia said.

"We were very happy," Caroline said.

"Did he pass away at home?"

The memory made Caroline tear up all over again. "No, at work. In his office. I had dropped by earlier to bring him lunch, which I often did. He was absolutely fine when I left. James, Julia's husband who worked with him at the law firm, found him slumped over his desk. He called the paramedics but by the time they arrived it was too late. It has been a huge shock."

Rosalia shook her head and sighed. "It makes no sense when bad things happen to good people. We have to believe that it's God's will."

Rosalia opened the drapes, and the light of the day lifted the dark mood. Outside the leaves of the olive trees shimmered in the sunlight.

"I hope you find your room comfortable," she said. "If you feel too warm just open the window. There is always a cool breeze at night."

Rosalia left her to freshen up.

Caroline was pleased that she understood everything that her aunt said in the Sardinian dialect. Her parents spoke in Italian in their home in America, but once Caroline had started school, she had switched to English. From then on, Caroline had refused to speak Italian to her parents. She wished that they had spoken English better. She had felt embarrassed when they had spoken in broken English in front of her friends. Caroline had made sure that they never visited her school, and she never told them about school events or parent teachers' conferences.

Caroline splashed cold water on her face and removed her makeup. Even though she was exhausted, she never went to bed without cleansing and moisturizing her skin. It paid off. Caroline looked younger than fifty-five; her smooth skin was unlined except for some laughter lines around her eyes. She was a striking woman. Her features, not perfect, her nose a tad too long, gave her an air of sophistication. Caroline was pleased that she didn't resemble her mother. She secretly thought that her mother, Claudia, was quite homely whereas her aunts Rosalia and Ornella were very attractive.

After Caroline unpacked her suitcase, she wrapped a towel around her body and walked barefoot down the passage to the bathroom. She glanced out of the window and saw Salvatore patting down the ground with a shovel where he had buried Chicco. She found it endearing that people took good care of their pets, even in death.

Caroline felt strange taking a shower with someone else's soaps and shampoos. A large loofah hung from the shower head. Two worn washcloths dangled from each hook. Caroline felt as if she was trespassing in a private sanctum and even the used bar of soap felt peculiar in her hands.

After her shower, dressed in her bathrobe, she made her way back to her room and was surprised to see Julia leaving her room.

"Hey, Jules, were you looking for me?" she said.

"I came to borrow your hairdryer. I couldn't find it."

Caroline found that strange; they had both bought dual voltage hairdryers for the trip.

Curled up in her comfortable bed, Caroline felt better about her decision to bring Julia along on the trip. She was determined to keep the connection that took so many years to build. It had not been easy. Julia had been rebellious as a teenager. Stuart had appreciated Caroline's efforts in keeping the family together by building a bond with his daughter. Now that he was gone, Caroline wanted to keep the relationship.

Chapter Two

A Visit to Her Mother

Caroline woke early to the sound of birds chirping and the clattering of dishes. When she walked into the kitchen, she saw that Rosalia was removing croissants from a white box tied with gold ribbon.

Rosalia looked up and smiled. "Good morning, my dearest niece. You are just in time for a freshly baked *cornetto*. Salvatore brought them back from the bakery."

Salvatore nodded in agreement.

Caroline took a cornetto and bit into it, then poured herself a cup of coffee from the silver jug on the stovetop. "I'm going to visit my mother at the nursing home," she said, in between bites.

"That's a wonderful idea. Just keep in mind that it's been two years since you've seen her in person, she has deteriorated," Rosalia said. "That is the unfortunate progression of the disease."

"I know," said Caroline, "I can see that on Facetime. It makes me so sad."

"You can be comforted that she is well cared for and quite happy. I visit her at least every other day."

Salvatore confirmed what she said. "Rosalia is an angel to your mama. She is the one who takes care of all her needs."

"And Ornella?" Caroline asked.

"Ornella is Ornella." He took a deep breath and let it out slowly, as if getting rid of troubled energy.

"Ornella is busy," Rosalia interjected. "They travel a lot. She is hardly in town."

Caroline picked up that this was a contentious topic. She changed the subject. "Well, I will be going then," she said. "Please tell Julia that I will be back around lunchtime."

Caroline left the house and walked towards the bus station. It was comforting to return to Oristano after some years and to find that the route was familiar because the landmarks never changed. She passed the church, then the bakery, the fruit shop, then turned left at the hair salon.

In Miami, the layout changed even though the seasons did not. Older buildings were torn down and modern ones erected in their place. Where a corner grocery store once stood, a multi-floor supermarket took its place. Old oceanfront motels were demolished to be replaced by glass and steel high-rise condos. Construction kept changing the landscape and everything familiar disappeared.

Caroline liked that she knew exactly where the pharmacy was and where the hair salon was that her aunts had frequented since they were young women. Even her favorite restaurants were in their original settings. She found the bus station in exactly the same place as it had been in her childhood.

Caroline took the bus to the edge of town to the assisted living home where her mother was staying. It wasn't a long walk from the bus stop but a difficult one. Not only was the steep gravel path taxing, but her emotional burden that wore her down. Each time she approached the large wrought iron gates with the sign *Sacro Cuore Degli Angeli*—Sacred Hearts of the Angels—a deep sadness washed over her.

Caroline punched in the code to the entrance and the gate swung open. She walked through the imposing wooden door and came to the reception desk. The lady at the desk hardly raised her head from the computer screen and if she recognized Caroline from the many previous visits, she didn't show it.

"I'm here to visit my mother, Signora Claudia Bellini," Caroline said.

Checking the daily programs on her screen, the middle-aged woman spoke. "You'll find her in the music room," she said.

"Thank you," said Caroline. She knew where the music room was. Caroline walked down the passage and turned left.

It was as though all the color had been sucked out of the room. A gray mist washed over the residents seated in their wheelchairs. A young man was playing the piano, but no one engaged with the music. Some stared into space concentrating on invisible objects while others scratched their heads or picked their noses. A number of caregivers dressed in white nursing scrubs leaned against the wall, as if they were at a party, and chatted to one another. They stopped talking when they noticed Caroline enter the room and walk towards her mother. They recognized her.

"*Ciao Mama*," she said gently kissing her forehead. Her mother did not move. She stared vacantly without acknowledging Caroline's presence.

A dark-haired caregiver dressed in a top and pants patterned with kittens and rainbows smiled at Caroline. She asked if she would like to take her mother back to her room.

Caroline nodded and wheeled her mother down the long passage to her room.

It was a small room, with a bed and night table with a lamp. A credenza held framed photos of Caroline as a child lined up like tin soldiers. There was a larger framed picture of her mother and father on their wedding day. A bay window let in natural light creating a rather cheerful atmosphere, broken only by the numerous pill bottles and bedside commode.

A nurse popped her head around the door. "Do you need any help, or would you like to be left alone?" she asked.

"I'm fine for now," Caroline said, "I'll be leaving in about an hour."

Caroline turned the wheelchair towards her so that she could look closely at her mother. Her mother had been a stocky woman, with a bland face and thick black hair. She looked nothing like her former self. She was fragile and pale with sunken eyes and straggly gray hair. Her eyes were clouded by cataracts and although her facial skin was surprisingly smooth, her hands gave away her age; they were wrinkled and arthritic. Her mother's sisters, similar in age, were still vibrant and filled with life. Caroline was saddened by this contrast. She thought that when the mind goes, so does the identity of the person.

Caroline did not look like other members of her family. She was fair, blue-eyed, tall and slim. She carried herself like an aristocrat whose passion was horse riding. Her mother, father, and her Aunt Rosalia were dark and exotic. But her Aunt Ornella was fair, and light-eyed too. Caroline dressed well in classic styles. She wore her highlighted blonde hair in a perfect bob. Although her face was angular, and her nose a little long, her ice blue eyes caught everyone's attention, She knew that she was a stunning woman.

Now, she spoke to her mother.

"Hello Mama," she said. She took her mother's hand and rubbed her fingers lightly over them. "This is Carolina," she said, "I am your daughter."

Her mother never moved.

Caroline wanted very much for her mother to show her some recognition. She bent down to her mother's level and pointed to her mother's chest. "Mama," she said clearly. Then Caroline pointed to herself and said, "*Figlia,* daughter." She repeated it.

Her mother shook her head. "*No,*" she said softly, "Ornella."

Caroline once again pointed to herself, "I am your daughter. Ornella is your sister." Her mother shut down, as if she was playing freeze dance when the music stopped.

"I love you, Mama," Caroline said. She pulled her chair closer, "I have some news to tell you. My husband, Stuart, died. You never liked him. You always said that he was too controlling of me. I am lonely. He has a daughter, Julia, but she doesn't like me." Caroline got up and poured herself a glass of water from a jug. "Do you want some water?"

She filled a glass with a small amount, then took one of the straws and held it to her mother's lips. She held her mother's chin with her other hand. The old lady sipped on the straw. When she stopped, she lifted her head and looked at Caroline. Caroline smiled and stroked her mother's hair. She thought she saw a glimmer of recognition in her mother's eyes, but perhaps it was wishful thinking.

Chapter Three

Things Are Not as They Seem

When Caroline arrived back at the house, she heard a lively conversation coming from the living room. Italian always fascinated her as a language; its lilting rhythm pleasing to the ear.

Caroline entered the room, and the conversation paused. All eyes turned on her.

"Ciao, Caroline!" said Rosalia, "look who came to see you!"

Caroline walked over and kissed Rosalia's daughter, Adela, on each cheek. She hadn't seen her cousin for a number of years and now Adela was grown up and married. Adela introduced her husband, Luca. It struck Caroline how wholesome the young couple looked. Fresh-faced, clear-eyed, and neatly dressed. As the afternoon progressed, this picture of health was marred by both Adela and Lucca periodically going to the patio to smoke.

Julia, who did not speak Italian, had no problems communicating; she was theatrical by nature. Her animated facial expressions, together with elaborate hand movements, made her intentions clear. Julia was a beautiful young woman. She was petite and slender, with abundant waist-length blonde hair. She carried herself with confidence, knowing her good looks won people over.

Caroline was proud of how much Julia had blossomed since Caroline had entered her life. Julia had been a chunky, dark-haired ten-year-old when Caroline and Stuart got married. After years of braces, a nose job, and weight reduction, Julia was transformed. She had focused on her psychological issues too, and she was in ongoing therapy to control her frequent rages. Her father had spared no money investing in his daughter's wellbeing and stability. At the age of eighteen, Stuart had agreed to fund her breast implants and liposuction. Stuart felt that it had paid dividends when Julia married James Callahan, an Ivy League law graduate with great potential.

"My husband is jealous that he couldn't come on this trip," Julia said to the family. "He would have loved to have met you all."

"I hear that he is a lawyer," said Salvatore.

"Yes, he is a partner in my late father's law firm. Thank God he is there to take over the reins since my father died."

"He will be a partner soon," Caroline interjected, "the other attorneys still have to vote him in."

"It's a given, Caroline," Julia said, annoyed. She asked Caroline, "Who do you think runs the whole company now? Ah, speak of the devil." Julia answered, then held up, her phone, the screen lighting up with a video image of a handsome young man. "This is my hubby, James."

They looked up. James was propped up in bed with a newspaper spread out in front of him.

"Hello," he called out, "nice to meet you all!"

Rosalia, Salvatore, Adela, and Luca waved back.

"Looks like you're having fun, Babe," he said to his wife. "I would have loved to be there, but someone has to work." He shrugged.

"Why aren't you at the office?" Julia asked.

"It's a public holiday."

"Oh, I forgot," she said.

"Where is he?" asked Luca.

"At home, in Florida."

"Hey Caroline!" James called out. "Take good care of my wife."

"Bye, Babe," said Julia. "Talk again soon. Love you!"

"I see your husband reads the English edition of '*The Sports Gazette*'," Luca said to Julia.

"Yes, he subscribes. He's a soccer nut, so he likes to keep up with the European teams."

"Oh, we will get along just fine," Luca said.

"How did you meet your husband?" asked Adela.

"Through my dad. James was fresh out of law school and was interning at my father's firm. One day, my father invited James for dinner at this fancy restaurant, and I pitched up by accident'," she said, laughing. "We had been planning it for weeks."

"You're lucky that your father wanted you to meet someone," said Adela. "My father, may he rest in peace, preferred me to stay single. No man was ever good enough for me."

"I guess I'm lucky that he died before I came along," said Luca.

"Oh, stop that," Adela said, "you treat me like a queen. That's all ever he wanted."

"Andiamo a mangiare, let's go eat," said Rosalia jumping up from the sofa.

The kitchen table was set with brown and yellow stoneware dishes on a yellow tablecloth. A vase of sunflowers in the center of the table complemented the colors. A steaming pot of tortellini in a clear broth bubbled on the stove.

Salvatore was on the back porch, grilling fish over an open fire. He looked up and waved. "Five more minutes," he mouthed.

He was a sturdy man, like a giant oak tree anchored in the ground. He wore his short gray hair combed back off his face; he was a handsome man who didn't have time for vanity. His philosophy was that idleness was close to a sin. Salvatore did not waste one second of the day. If he wasn't taking care of his fruit and vegetable garden, he was mending fences and painting the house. He rarely bought things for the house. He preferred to make everything by hand. The only place that wasn't his domain was the kitchen. He enjoyed grilling but it was his wife, Rosalia, who wore the crown of *il capocuoco,* top chef of the house.

Caroline envied her aunt's relaxed manner of entertaining. Rosalia had the gift of making everyone feel welcome in her home. When last minute guests arrived, she was happy. 'The more the merrier' she would say. Rosalia could whip up a delicious meal using the ingredients she had at hand. It helped that their garden was always filled with vegetables and salad ingredients waiting to be picked. Herbs like basil, chives, parsley and mint were just a snip away.

When Caroline entertained Stuart's colleagues for dinner, she was so anxious that she couldn't sleep the night before. Even family and close friends visiting stressed her out. She overthought everything. What if there wasn't enough to eat? What if the food didn't taste good? What if someone had allergies? It didn't help that Stuart's ex-wife, though not loyal, was an excellent cook. Julia would bring that up at almost every meal. *My mother's roast chicken was amazing. Yours I can't eat.* Stuart never admonished his daughter, so Julia accepted it as the truth. Stuart h ad finally put a stop to inviting company over to their home. He told his wife that it wasn't worth the anxiety it caused. He insisted on hosting guests at a restaurant. It was very rare that anyone visited their beautiful home anymore.

Luca and Adela got up to leave. "Luca has a busy day tomorrow," Adela said. "He has to be up very early to deliver wine to the restaurants."

Caroline rose from the table and attempted to help wash the dishes.

"No, no," Rosalia admonished. "Salvatore and I will do it – it's easier that way." She turned her head to face Caroline. "How is mama doing?"

"She seems to be okay. I have noticed a big change in two years. The saddest part is that she doesn't seem to recognize me anymore."

Rosalia bent her head. "I know. I don't think that she recognizes me anymore either."

"She did call me Ornella. I think she confused me with her."

Rosalia ran the dishes under the tap, rinsing them off with a cloth. She then stacked them on the side. "Losing one's mind is the biggest punishment," she said. "Out of us three sisters your mother was the liveliest. She was the first to go up on the dance floor and dance all night. The boys were crazy about her."

"I didn't know that," said Caroline, "she always seemed so quiet."

Rosalia clapped her hands. "Let's think of happier things," she said. "Tomorrow, we will take you and Julia for an authentic Sardinian dinner at Mama Sofia's Trattoria. Aunt Ornella and Uncle Beppe are in town. Their boat is docked at Porto Cervo. They can't wait to see you."

"I can't wait to see them!" Caroline answered. She turned to Julia who was scrolling on her phone. "Some of my favorite childhood memories are of spending time with my aunt and uncle. They had a fabric factory, and they would let me cut up materials to make clothes for my dolls."

Julia was not impressed. She stood up and walked out of the room.

"She must be missing her husband," said Rosalia.

"Pay no attention to her," said Caroline, "she is a moody girl."

Back in her room, Caroline could hear the comfortable banter between her aunt and Salvatore as they were cleaning up the kitchen. She unpacked her vanity case and realized that she had a dual voltage electric brush that could be used to dry and style hair. Caroline thought that would be perfect for Julia. She grabbed her robe and carried the brush across the stone floor and up the stairs to the apartment where Julia was staying. When she approached the closed door, she could hear Julia talking. She leaned close.

"Babe, I almost died when I saw you in the hotel bed this evening. You know that I was going to Facetime you. You are supposed to be in Florida, not here. Literally the point of the call was to prove that, and you left the newspaper out."

Caroline froze. *What are they saying? Is James in Oristano pretending to be back in the States?* She had not recognized the room on the phone call. It wasn't their house in Miami.

"James, listen, we can't fuck up. When we Facetime, you have to make sure that it looks like you're at home."

Why would James be in Sardinia? Caroline pressed her ear to the door.

"Okay, keep in touch. It's so weird that you are just around the corner. Miss you too, love you." Julia ended the call.

Caroline made her way silently down the steps, tiptoeing to her room. Her heart was beating loudly, and her hands shook so badly that she could hardly open the door. Something weird was going on.

Chapter Four

Fresh Baked Pastries

The church bells chimed six times and woke Caroline, it took her a few moments to remember where she was. There was something comforting about church bells. They rang on the hour consistently, no matter what was happening in one's life. The church bells were the background music to the lives of the people who lived in Oristano so that they didn't pay attention to them anymore, but Caroline noticed the bells ringing loud and clear, marking the passing of each hour.

Caroline stirred, and the events of the night before came into her mind. A feeling of unease washed over her. Julia and James were up to something. If she confronted Julia, she would just deny everything and make out that Caroline was imagining things. Julia had a way of doing that. There were times when Julia had blatantly lied to her father about

Caroline and Stuart would often take Julia's side. It had hurt Caroline very much.

Caroline got out of bed, put on her robe and walked down the hallway to wash up.

Rosalia, dressed in a pink floral dress, was in the kitchen making breakfast. Just as with the church bells, Rosalia's days had a set rhythm that gave her purpose. She greeted each day with joy and intention. The most mundane tasks gave her satisfaction, even washing the dishes. She scrubbed off the leftover food with brisk movements, then rinsed the dishes, methodically, in the running water. It was as if she was moving to a silent waltz. Rosalia stacked each plate on the rack to dry, running her fingers lightly over their rims as if bidding them farewell until the next time. When Rosalia sliced onions or tomatoes she pushed the knife down with firm, precise motions so that each slice was the same thickness and size. Every household chore was done with joy. Making up the beds was approached as if she was conducting her personal orchestra. Firstly, she pulled the sheets up with gusto, allowing them to float like clouds before falling back onto the bed. She then tucked the sheets back into the frame patting them as if they were her favorite pets.

On this morning, Caroline found her aunt removing puff pastries from a ribboned box and placing each one like a precious jewel onto plates.

"Good morning, Caroline," she said, "Salvatore just brought these back from the bakery, fresh from the oven."

It was Salvatore's daily ritual to head to the bakery first thing in the morning.

"They look, and smell, wonderful," said Caroline.

"I used to make my own, but my husband insists on buying readymade. He says that I spend too much time in the kitchen."

"It's true," Salvatore interjected from where he was hidden behind the sports page of the daily newspaper. He took a sip of coffee and reached across the table to pick up a cornetto filled with cream. "I had to show Rosalia, that there is more to life, then cooking and cleaning."

"But amore," said Rosalia to her husband, "I don't see *you* ever taking a break." Rosalia cocked her head to the side. "Salvatore and I have the same philosophy, if we are not busy doing something, then we fear that we are wasting the day."

Salvatore poured himself a cup of espresso and gulped it down. "You know, maybe we are doing too much," he said to his wife. "We are not getting any younger. It may be a good idea to slow down. We should practice *dolce far niente,* the sweetness of doing nothing. I think we have earned it. Don't you agree?"

"I don't see the housework as a chore – it's my pleasure. I'm not sure that I can sit around looking at the sunset." Rosalia laughed.

"I agree," said Caroline. "Our lives are too structured and pressured. Stuart was all about work and no play. I tried to help him find a balance. I begged him to travel with me and he promised that he was winding down. Then it was too late."

"So sad. He died too young," said Salvatore.

Julia entered the kitchen and joined the conversation. "My father worked his butt off and now he is gone."

"He gave us a wonderful life," said Caroline. "Dad was able to give you everything you needed and wanted. You never had to worry about a thing." She poured Julia a cup of coffee then placed a pastry in front of her.

"I guess so," Julia answered. She bit into a flaky *sfogliatella* that left a circle of white powder around her mouth. She looked at Caroline and said, "Let's just say that *you* never have to worry about money again. Me not so much."

Julia's phone buzzed. It was James on Facetime. "Hi Babe," she said, "we are having breakfast. The yummiest pastries." She pointed the camera at the plate of pastries for him to see.

"Looks delicious," he said, "I'm jealous."

"That's your fault. You could have come with, so don't be jealous now," she said. "I begged you to come to Italy, but no, you were too swamped at the office."

"Hey Caroline!" James called out.

"Hi," she said. "Why are you up so early? It must be dawn over there?"

"I'm off to the gym," he said. "Speaking of health, don't let my wife get fat from all those pastries."

Julia got up from her seat, "Babe, let me show you around the house," she said. "It's very Italian. Simple and unassuming."

Caroline thought that it was rude of Julia to take James on a tour of the house. Since she had discovered that James was in town, she couldn't shake the icy feeling that spread over her now. Caroline decided not to confront Julia yet. She knew their secret and now had the upper hand. But she couldn't grasp what they were up to.

"He looks like a nice guy," said Salvatore. "Next time bring him with you."

"Since my dad died, James has taken care of the business," Julia said as she paced around showing James the rest of the kitchen. "He has to make sure that everything is running smoothly at the law firm," she added.

"Excuse my curiosity," said Salvatore, "does James own the company now?"

Julia stopped filming and hung up the phone. "

He will in the future," she said.

Caroline cleared her throat. "I own the company now," she interjected.

Julia looked at Caroline sharply. "Let's just say that you are very fortunate to have James in control." She stuck out her chin. "What do you know about running a law firm?"

Caroline seethed but kept her thoughts to herself. There was no way that she was going to give up control of the company.

Rosalia changed the subject. "I will tidy up and you two get ready," she said to Caroline and Julia. "At midday we are meeting up with my sister Ornella and Beppe for lunch at Mama Sofia's trattoria."

"Lunch? There is no way I can eat a big lunch so soon after breakfast," said Julia.

"You will love my Aunt Ornella and her husband. They are great. Larger than life," said Caroline.

"Do I have to go?" said Julia. "I would rather go to the beach than hang out with your family."

"Please Julia, I would like you to meet them. I paid for your flight here so the least you can do is meet my family."

"She's such a bitch," Julia said, through her teeth.

Chapter Five

The Accadis

Giuseppe and Ornella Accadi were part of Sardinian society. In fact, they were the backbone of Sardinian society. Beppe's lineage was an old, established Sardinian family who manufactured fabric. He had inherited the factory from his father after he died, and had since expanded the company, supplying retail stores found in most of Italy's larger cities.

Claudia, Rosalia and Ornella were the daughters of hardworking middle-class parents who owned a small jewelry store in Oristano. They had a loyal following of customers due to their reputation for honesty and fair prices. When Beppe, short for Guiseppe, started courting their youngest daughter, Ornella, her parents were very pleased. Both her older sisters were already married, one with a child. Ornella was in her early twenties, which was considered old for marriage at that time. Ornella was a beautiful girl, prettier than her sisters, but there was one small problem; she had a *reputation*. Ornella was a free spirit and the boys in town took advantage of her generosity. They had fun with her but when it came to settling down with a wife, they preferred a more serious girl.

Signor and Signora Accadi were not happy with their son Beppe's choice of bride. They had hoped that their son would marry into a more successful and refined Sardinian family. A jeweler, in their minds, was not a suitable match for the wealthy Accadi name. Beppe was destined to take over the family's fabric company and their opinion was that Ornella was not good enough for their son. They soon realized that the more pressure they put on their son to part ways with Ornella, the more obstinate he became. "I love her," he told them. "I have to follow my heart and that's my final word."

Beppe married Ornella in a simple wedding ceremony and his parents chose not to be present. This hurt the young couple and even though Beppe took over his father's fabric company, his parents never accepted his wife.

Despite not coming from money, Ornella had excellent taste in clothes. She dressed impeccably. The young couple lived a lavish and golden lifestyle, but a dark cloud hung over their heads. Ornella had trouble falling pregnant. The doctors were baffled, both Ornella and Beppe were physically capable of having a child, but months led into years, and nothing happened. The young couple visited a top infertility clinic in Switzerland and after tests and procedures, Ornella still did not conceive. All her friends were having babies and although she put on a happy face for them, inside she was burning with envy. She became the best aunt to her niece Carolina and spoiled her with all the toys money could buy but a sadness was always present in her heart.

She felt a failure as a woman and a wife. Ornella wasn't able to give her husband his lifelong dream, a son. Instead, they acquired two little Yorkie puppies, a girl and a boy whom they named Remy and Lily.

Ornella overindulged them like surrogate children. She dressed them in little matching outfits and pushed them in a baby carriage around the town. In the beginning, Beppe ignored the puppies until one day, Lily choked on a chicken bone and almost died. When Ornella called to tell him that the vet said that things were not looking good for her, suddenly Beppe's heart was pierced by an arrow of regret. He jumped into his Lamborghini and raced straight to the vet.

"I don't care what it costs!" he cried as he ran through the door. "You have to save my baby."

Ornella was confused. Beppe always complained that the dogs were a nuisance and impacted their lives negatively. He griped about the fact that they couldn't travel without a nanny for the dogs, that they had to fly in special fresh meat from the mainland for their meals, and about the expense of the groomer who came weekly to their house. Beppe was annoyed at how much Ornella indulged them. But when he was confronted with Lily's mortality, he flew into a panic.

"Ornella, who is the patron saint of animals?" he shouted to his wife.

"San Francesco d'Assisi," she answered.

Beppe got down on his knees and clasped his hands in prayer. The vet coughed and looked away. Beppe's prayers were answered, Lily rallied and recovered. From that day on, he did not want Ornella to push them in the carriage any longer, he insisted on carrying them, one under each arm.

Ornella even as an older woman was still a beauty. Petite in size but tall in spirit. She carried herself straight, shoulders pulled back and head held high. This gave her the appearance of a taller woman. She wore her hair silver hair pulled back in a low chignon. Her fair skin highlighted her almond shaped blue eyes. Ornella had worshipped the sun her whole life and still did. Her smooth, unlined face belied the universal theory of the sun's harmful rays. Beppe, on the other hand, was reptilian. He was tanned but his skin was craggy. With his striking blue eyes and shock of white hair he stood out in the crowd. The exotic couple turned heads wherever they went. They appeared to be the perfect couple. However, there was a tiny flaw that marred the illusion. Beppe had a roving eye. He was drawn to beautiful women and could not resist the temptation. All his dalliances were with much younger women, whom he told upfront that he loved his wife. Though there was no future for these relationships, he would compensate the women financially and they were satisfied with the arrangement. Ornella turned a blind eye to her husband's dalliances as long as there were no emotional ties. However, life is not always black and white, and Beppe committed the cardinal sin, he fell in love with one of his flings. She was the most unlikely choice of all. Laura was in her late thirties, ten years older than his prior flirtations, and she wasn't even that pretty. She looked like the average girl next door. She wore no make-up, and her hair was usually tied back in a ponytail. She wore t-shirts and jeans. But the most remarkable thing of all is that she had two young children, a boy and a girl, both under ten years old.

Beppe confessed his feelings for Laura to his wife, and this time Ornella knew things were different.

"I am going to set up an apartment for Laura and her children," Beppe said at breakfast.

Ornella bit her lower lip and twisted her wedding ring. "I will not tolerate that," she said.

His jaw tightened. "This is how it's going to be."

"I cannot accept that," said Ornella. "What about my reputation in this town?"

"Either you accept the situation, or we will have to get a divorce." Beppe's face was grim, and his eyes turned to stone.

Ornella glowered at him. She choked on a strawberry that she had been eating. The butler came forward and hit her firmly on the back. He then poured her a glass of water.

"You are important to me," said Beppe, "and so is Laura. Don't make me choose, because you will regret it."

Ornella's eyes flashed. She jumped up and ran out of the room. Their housemaid became so nervous that she dropped a bottle of water on the floor. Moments later, she frantically vacuumed up the broken glass.

Signor Accadi explained to the maid, "The Signora is dramatic. What is the big deal? In some cultures, men have a few wives. I'm not asking for that – just a mistress. What is the fuss?"

The maid who knew her boss intimately, nodded.

Ornella had no option but to accept the situation. Beppe bought her a sizeable diamond pendant, and Laura and her children were set up in an apartment close by.

The nights when Beppe was missing, Ornella would fall asleep after drinking copious amounts of wine followed by her sleeping pills. She insisted on two rules; number one was *discretion*. She made Beppe promise that their family and friends would never see him and his mistress together and number two was that he had to be back home showered and shaved in time for breakfast.

Beppe was permitted to take two vacations per year with his mistress, but Ornella didn't want to know any of the details.

"Beppe is on a business trip," she told her friends. The only ones she confided in were her sisters, Rosalia and Claudia. They saw her tears on many occasions.

"*Tesoro*, darling," Rosalia advised her. "There are two things you can do – leave him or pretend it's not happening."

The latter is what Ornella chose to do. She saw no future as a middle-aged divorcée, so she stayed living her comfortable life with bitterness and regret.

Chapter Six

Mama Sofia's Trattoria

When the Arcadis walked into Mama Sofia's Trattoria, it was akin to royalty arriving. Mama Sofia rushed out of the kitchen to greet them. "Welcome esteemed friends!" she cried. It was an honor that they graced her restaurant with their presence. Rosalia had called the night before to make sure that the Accadis' favorite dish *Porcetto arrosto*, roast pork, was on the menu. Mama Sofia and her daughter Tina roasted the suckling pig before the sun came up.

Salvatore, Rosalia, Adela, Luca, Caroline and Julia were seated at a corner table. They all jumped up to greet the Accadis, except Julia who was posting selfies on her phone. Beppe and Ornella were not overly effusive by nature and while the family was bursting with happiness to see them, they each offered a cool cheek to be kissed. Once seated, Ornella hugged Caroline. She had always had a soft spot for her niece since she was a child. She had doted on

Caroline when she was growing and took her shopping or out to lunch. When Caroline and her family left to live in America, Ornella had been devastated. She had missed her sister, Claudia, but she had missed her niece even more.

Ornella acknowledged Julia with a nod. She peered at her with half-shut eyes and in one swoop took in the labeled attire, Prada sunglasses, Versace dress and Bottega Veneto bag.

The first words that Julia said to Ornella were, "I heard you have a boat." She cocked her head to the side. "Where is it docked?"

"A yacht," Ornella corrected her. "We keep it in the marina at Porto Cervo."

"That's super cool," Julia said, "I've always wanted to have a boat, but my father was not the boating type. Do you have a picture?"

Ornella shrugged. "I don't carry around photos of our yacht. I do have a photo of Caroline and her mother when they were younger. Would you like to see it?"

Julia took a sip of her wine "Not really, your family is not my family, so I don't really know who's who."

The restaurant was filling up with regulars who had their assigned tables for their daily lunch. They were mostly made up of local office workers who spent two hours over lunch before heading home for a nap and then returning back to work for the evening hours.

Mama Sofia brought out large platters of antipasti: sliced salamis, grilled peppers, roasted artichokes and *bruschetta*

– grilled rounds of bread, piled high with chopped tomato, basil and olive oil.

"Today, my friends, we have your favorite. Roast pork is the main course, prepared exactly how you like it," Mama Sofia announced with glowing pride.

Ornella looked up at Mama Sofia. "Beppe and I are taking a break from meat for a while."

"Since when?" said Beppe.

"Since today," Ornella said. Turning back to Mama Sofia she asked, "What fish do you have?"

Without missing a beat Mama Sofia said, "We have grilled langoustines, and sea bass, straight off the boat." Her voice quivered with disappointment.

"That's perfect," said Ornella. "Bring us both."

"Salvatore and I will have the pork," said Rosalia, "it's always a treat."

"For us too," said Adela.

Mama Sofia looked at Julia.

"Do you speak English?" Julia asked.

"A little."

"What do you have that doesn't have any carbs?"

"*Mi scusi?* Excuse me?" said Mama Sofia.

"Can I have the meat sauce from the spaghetti but minus the spaghetti?" Julia asked, firmly.

Mama Sofia looked at Rosalia for an interpretation.

"Only the ragu, no pasta," said Rosalia.

Mama Sofia nodded her head; she was disappointed.

"And no garlic please," Julia added. "I'm allergic to garlic."

When it was Caroline's turn to order, she said, "I will have whatever you want to bring me. Everything is delicious."

Beppe was irritated by the lengthy menu discussions. He got up from the table and went outside to the balcony. Ornella craned her neck; she could see him talking on his phone.

She nudged Rosalia and whispered, "*deve parlare con las puttana.* He must be talking to the whore."

Rosalia squeezed her sister's hand. "Pay no attention," she said.

When the food was on the table, Beppe came back in.

"You took so long now your food is cold," said Ornella.

"That's okay," he answered. "I like my food cold."

"That's news to me," said Ornella. "How many times do you complain at home, then we have to reheat your food."

"Are you looking for an argument?" Beppe said.

"Don't take your calls from your girlfriend when you are out with me," she hissed.

Beppe jumped up abruptly and his chair came crashing to the floor.

"Don't start Ornella!" he shouted. "Can't we have one nice dinner together?" He stormed out.

The restaurant became silent, the only sound were the knives and forks hitting the plates.

Salvatore raised his glass. "Let's enjoy this wonderful meal."

Ornella patted down her hair and re-applied her lipstick. "I guess you now have to give me a ride home," she said to

Rosalia. She knew where her husband would be sleeping that night. With his mistress.

"Are we still going on the boat tomorrow?" asked Caroline.

"Of course," said Ornella. "Life goes on." She nudged Rosalia. "This too shall pass. The captain and crew are preparing for two days at sea. I believe the food has already been ordered."

"Can we bring anything?" said Salvatore. "Whiskey, cigars?"

"Just bring yourselves," said Ornella. "Pack lightly."

Salvatore turned to Caroline. "Your stepdaughter is in for a treat. It's fun on the yacht."

"I call her my bonus-daughter, not *step*," said Caroline patting Julia's hand.

Julia pulled her hand away and shifted in her seat. "I wish you wouldn't," she said annoyed. "I'm not your daughter; I *am* your stepdaughter. Say it like it is."

Caroline swallowed and looked hurt.

"Who care about labels?" said Salvatore. "Love is love."

Chapter Seven

A Boat Trip Sounds Like Fun

Salvatore parked the van in front of the house. Rosalia sat up front, Caroline and Julia sat in the back with their luggage in the trunk. As they wound along the rugged coastline, Caroline felt her head clear. The narrow twisting roads were terrifying, but Caroline had faith in Salvatore's driving. Years of experience had taught him how to navigate the oncoming traffic in precarious spaces with confidence. Even though the drop from the road to the ocean below was treacherous, Caroline felt calm. Julia on the other shut her eyes tightly.

"I can't look," she said, "this is worse than any rollercoaster I've ever been on."

They arrived at the Marina at Porto Cervo before midday. Boats of different sizes lined up against the jetty. Flags flying from the stern of the yachts indicated which countries they originated from.

"There she is!" Salvatore announced, pointing to the largest one. A majestic white orb of perfection was docked close by. 'Ornella' was painted in navy and gold letters along the hull. Salvatore pulled up and parked close to the walkway.

"Wow, this is some yacht!" Julia exclaimed. "I have to show James." She immediately took out her phone and Facetimed him.

It was impressive. There were eight cabin windows on the lower level and a ramp leading up to an expansive open deck. At the top of the ramp the captain and first officer, both dressed in white uniforms, welcomed the guests. Caroline, familiar with the boat from previous visits, was still in awe of its beauty and size. Ornella stood beside the welcoming crew in a pink and white caftan that fluttered like sails in the breeze.

"Welcome, welcome," she said. "For the next two days this is your floating home."

"Thank you," the guests said in unison.

"It's very gracious of you and Beppe to invite us," Salvatore added.

Caroline kissed her aunt on both cheeks, then she shook the captain's hand. She glanced at the ocean to check if it was calm. She was not a good sailor; rough seas made her sick.

"Good morning, everyone," the captain announced, "welcome to the Ornella." He cleared his throat and spoke in a serious tone. "We will be leaving port in two hours and heading into the ocean. Tomorrow at 13:00 hours we will drop anchor for a day of swimming, snorkeling and fun in the ocean." He looked at the guests one by one, as though mentally summing them up. "If there is anything my crew or I can do for you, please don't hesitate to ask."

The captain was perfectly cast, like an actor playing a captain. He even sported a neat grey beard and mustache.

"Graziella will show you to your cabins," Ornella said. "You can settle in and then we will have a little lunch. As soon as the captain is ready, he will blow the horn, and we will head out to sea."

Julia clapped her hands and broke into a little jig. "This is so exciting!" she said. "Look James," she said into her phone, "isn't this a dream come true?"

Caroline told her to put her phone away. "It's rude," she said. Caroline was appalled at the way Julia believed she was fooling all of them. Well she wasn't fooling Caroline.

The smile on Julia's face faded as she turned her phone off.

The open deck had lots of plush seating for passengers to sit and watch the sea go by. There was a large oval white table with matching chairs under an awning where, weather permitting, the meals were served. The back deck had a small dipping pool with rows of deck chairs. There was also a bubbling hot tub and a ping-pong table. In the corner, a full-service bar was set up. No detail for an enjoyable cruise was left out.

Graziella, in white uniform, led the four guests to their cabins. They passed a lounge area furnished in taupe and beige. Each cabin was lavishly furnished and with a floor-to-ceiling window overlooking the sea and had its own bathroom. Rosalia and Salvatore shared a cabin but Caroline and Julia each had their own.

"Where is the Accadi suite?" Julia asked Graziella.

"On the upper level," said Graziella.

"It is possible for me to have a cabin up there too?" she asked. "I get claustrophobic."

"Unfortunately, not. That is the only suite on the top floor."

A crease formed between her brows. "Are you a 100% sure?" Julia said. "I passed a cabin when I went to the bathroom up there."

Graziella's jaw tightened. "That's for the signora's clothes. No guests are allowed there."

Julia shrugged. "That's a little over the top," she said.

As soon as Caroline entered her cabin, she unpacked her small carry-on and placed her toiletries in the bathroom. Most of the beauty essentials were already there and she was impressed by the thoughtful selection. She sat on the bed and marveled at the accommodation. Since the last time that she and Stuart were on the boat, the cabins had been remodeled. Everything was sleek, clean and light. Pure luxury. Every detail had been thought of, from bottled water and wine in the mini fridge, to the Frette cotton robe in the bathroom. The only thing that marred her happiness was that Stuart was no longer with her to enjoy this. She took a deep breath and counted her blessings, focusing on the positive things in her life.

The group reconvened in the dining room on the upper deck where a buffet lunch was set out. Beppe, dressed from top to toe in beige, cut a very elegant figure. He wore linen slacks with a loose-fitting linen shirt unbuttoned, to show off his healthy tan. His soft suede loafers completed his image as master of the yacht. Beppe welcomed his guests warmly. The silver bangles on his wrists jangled as he hugged the guests. He put his arm around his wife as if she was the love of his life. There wasn't a shred of animosity from the previous day.

A steward passed a tray of mimosas around. Everyone took a flute.

"Can I have just plain champagne?" said Julia, "I don't like it mixed with orange juice."

"Of course," said the steward. "Champagne coming up immediately."

They took their seats around the table. There was an abundance of salads and cold seafood laid out and the diners could also order hot options from the daily menu.

Lobster salad, egg salad, smoked salmon, caviar and blinis were just a few of the choices. Grilled steaks, fish, hamburgers and bouillabaisse were always available for lunch. Alcoholic and nonalcoholic beverages were available 24/7.

There was a loud blast from the horn as the boat left the dock. "We are moving," Salvatore said. "*Questo e la vita!* This is life," he said, raising his glass.

"Are you going to swim in the ocean when we drop anchor tomorrow?" Julia asked Caroline.

Caroline shook her head, "Not me. I can't swim."

"How can you say that?" said Julia, "I've seen you swimming."

"Well, I can kind of float," said Caroline. "I don't think I'm good enough to swim in the deep sea." Caroline wondered at Julia's insistence; why wasn't she asking anyone else?

The chief officer announced to the group that they would be at sea for the rest of the day and night but would drop anchor the following morning, weather permitting, for some fun and swimming.

The chief stewardess added that dinner would be served on the upper deck at 20:00. She announced in perfect English, "On behalf of your esteemed hosts Signor and Signora Accadi, the captain and staff, we wish you a pleasant and enjoyable sailing."

Ornella had changed into a gold bikini and lay on a lounge chair facing the sun. She was a woman of an advanced age, and her body showed it. Although slender, her skin was no longer firm, and it was loose and crepey. Her stomach spilled over her minuscule bikini bottom like melting ice-cream. Ornella clearly did not lack self-esteem; she appeared to be happy with her body as it was. She paid no attention to the opinion of others.

"How can she wear a bikini?" Julia whispered behind her hand to Caroline. "It's gross."

"It's great," said Caroline, "European women are far more self-confident than we are. They don't care what other people think. We could learn a lesson from them."

"I disagree," said Julia, "a one piece would look more elegant." She took a sip of champagne. "*Please* swim with me tomorrow. It will be fun."

"I'm afraid of the water," said Caroline, "I always worry what's lurking beneath, besides I'm not a good swimmer."

"Ornella said that they have kickboards and noodles down there. The lower deck has a launch pad into the water. Beppe said they have wave runners too. The crew will be there to help."

"It's not my thing. You go and enjoy."

"Please Caroline, take the plunge, pun intended." She smiled. "You always lecture me about stepping out of one's comfort zone. Practice what you preach."

The next morning the sky was blue, and the sea was calm. Breakfast was set up on the middle deck under a canvas canopy. Coffee and freshly squeezed orange juice were available on the long table and so were scrambled eggs, croissants, sourdough bread, platters of cheese, and cold cuts. Sliced melon, peaches, kiwi fruit and mango filled glass platters.

"Can I please have champagne?" said Julia to the steward. "French. No Italian crap."

Ornella and Rosalia chatted together in the Sardinian dialect as if it were their secret language. Their sisterly bond was firm. Caroline watched them having fun and she wished that her mother was able to join them. She felt sad that her mother was not able to recognize her family any longer. She thought of her in the memory care facility, struggling with Alzheimer's. Caroline had considered bringing her mother to the States, but the cost of assisted living over there was much higher than where she was. It was Stuart who nixed the idea; he said that Caroline's mother would be happier near her sisters. They did visit her regularly and Caroline came to visit as often as she could, even though her mother did not know who she was any longer.

The two brothers-in-law, Salvatore and Beppe, got along well. Since Salvatore and Rosalia had married later in life, the two couples spent a lot of time together. Rosalia was happy with their camaraderie because usually when one marries for the second time after the death of a spouse, the new spouse is not always welcomed with open arms. Salvatore and Rosalia had been married almost seven years, and they were grateful to have discovered a new lease of life.

Beppe was not an easy man to get along with. He had a strong personality and liked things to go his way. He had been a tough boss who barked orders at his workers at the factory. He called it '*delegare*', delegating, but since retiring, he had not lost his bossy persona. There were only two people who he couldn't boss around – his wife Ornella and his new brother-in-law Salvatore.

Salvatore, a retired engineer, had been in charge of important projects for the Italian government. He was highly respected by his peers. While both of them suffered no fools, Salvatore was kinder and more compassionate than Beppe who could be abrupt and rude. The two men had heated discussions on politics and world events and, although they didn't always agree with one another, they respected each other's opinion. Only when it came to soccer would all hell broke loose. Both were loyal fans to their teams and would not budge on their opinions.

The two men were watching a soccer match on the TV when the captain announced on the loudspeaker that he was dropping anchor. They paid him no attention.

The captain warned the guests that even though the water was calm they must stay mindful and not swim far from the boat.

Caroline and Julia went down in their bathing suits to the lower deck. When Caroline saw the calm, turquoise ocean, she was tempted to abandon her fears and jump in. Antonio, one of the crew showed them how to put on their snorkels and flippers. He gave Caroline a demonstration of spitting on the facemask to clear any fog. He instructed her how to breathe with the snorkel. Julia was an experienced snorkeler and didn't need any coaching.

"I'm such a baby," Caroline said. "I'm so nervous."

Antonio calmed her fears. "There is nothing to worry about," he said, "I will stand right here and if you need me, I will jump in and help you."

Caroline and Julia put their flippers on, and Antonio demonstrated how to fall backwards from the ledge in the water. When both women were in the water, he handed Caroline a kickboard to make her feel more confident and in control.

The water was calm and once Caroline relaxed and stopped hyperventilating, she began breathing evenly. Soon she was able to view colorful schools of fish swimming around them. She even started enjoying herself. Caroline gently kicked her feet and swam alongside Julia. She felt exhilarated and as her confidence grew, the fear dissipated, and she focused on the beauty of nature surrounding her.

When Julia tapped her on the shoulder and gestured that they should go back to the boat, Caroline was shocked by how far out they had swum. She turned to look back. The boat was a tiny speck; they were much farther out than she had realized. They started swimming back. Caroline held onto the kickboard and kicked gently, but soon the water turned rough, and she became tired. Her breathing was labored and her legs felt heavy. The more she kicked the more tired she became, until she felt too exhausted to go further. Caroline tried to communicate with Julia, but she was advancing ahead with long strokes. It became obvious to Caroline that Julia was deliberately leaving her behind. Caroline registered the distance to the boat and felt momentary panic.

Finally, Caroline made it to the boat, just in time to see Julia hauling herself up onto the deck. Caroline panicked. Where was the ladder? She tried to hoist herself up onto the deck, but her body felt like a dead weight, and she flailed in the water. Caroline lifted her mask off her face and cried out for help. There was no one there but Julia who was obliviously drying off with a towel. Just as Caroline felt she might not be able to hold on any longer, Julia finally noticed her, and she ran to the edge of the deck and reached out her hand. Caroline almost managed to hoist herself up, but she lost her grip and fell back into the water. The water was rough, and the boat tilted from side to side.

Caroline tried to scream for Julia to come closer to the edge, but the words couldn't come out of her mouth. The rocking of the boat added to her exhaustion and soon she started swallowing water. The last thing Caroline saw was Julia's face peering over the edge as she sank into the water. It was the same expression that Julia had whenever she got her own way. *Why would Julia be smug?* was Caroline's last thought as she sank deeper.

When Caroline opened her eyes, she was lying on the deck with Antonio pressing on her chest, water ejected from her mouth as she vomited.

"Thank God, I arrived just in time," Antonio said. I pulled you out of the water. What happened? Never mind. Just concentrate on breathing." He was shaking. "Call the coast guard!" he cried out.

The captain called for help. Beppe ran around in circles with his hands over his head.

Ornella shouted, "I knew this was a bad idea!"

Julia sat on the edge of the deck, with her legs dangling over the water filming the scene on her phone.

A water ambulance pulled up alongside the yacht and three medics jumped out. They stabilized Caroline and wrapped her in an aluminum blanket.

"We have to take her back for observation to the hospital," one of them said.

They carried her on a gurney and placed her in the small boat and raced back to shore.

Caroline spent the night in the local hospital. The doctor told her that she was lucky to be alive. When she lay in bed in the dark hospital room the vision of her reaching for Julia's hand played over and over in her mind. A terrible thought haunted her. *Did Julia purposely pull her hand away?* Caroline was convinced that was what happened. Caroline was too tired to think any further and she fell into a deep sleep but in her dreams, it became even clearer; it had not been an accident.

Chapter Eight

The Bellini Sisters

When they were younger, the three sisters, Claudia, Rosalia and Ornella Bellini, lived with their parents in a small house at the edge of Oristano. Like most of the houses in the area, theirs was over two hundred years old and built like a fort. The gray stone was polished smoothly from years of the elements: sun, rain, and wind. The Bellini girls were known around town for their beauty. The two older ones had dark, almond shaped eyes, olive skin, slim bodies and waist- length hair. Ornella, the youngest, was different. She was fair-skinned and blue-eyed. Her golden hair was long and wavy. Ornella looked like a storybook princess and acted like one. Her older sisters doted on her and spoiled her with love. Their mother had no favorites, all three of her daughters were a blessing from heaven; but her father did. He was bitterly disappointed when his wife gave birth to a third daughter. He had hoped and prayed for a son. All his dreams of teaching his son to go hunting and play soccer were dashed. In the beginning, he could hardly look at the newborn. But slowly, as she started to smile and make eye contact with him, his heart softened. It wasn't long before he called her *my golden girl* and, even if he didn't say it, Ornella became his favorite child.

Signor Bellini owned the only jewelry store in town, and he made sure that his wife and daughters never lacked for gold and diamond jewelry.

Once the three sisters finished high school, they were expected to get married. Claudia, the smartest of all three, asked her parents if she could go on to study further. She wanted to be a schoolteacher.

"No," said her father. "Education is wasted on girls. You need to find a husband, get married, and have children."

"But dear," Signora Bellini argued, "Claudia can do both. There are girls who are married, have children and work in the mornings."

"Not my daughters," he said firmly. "My answer is final."

Oristano was a small community where most people knew each other.

"Your daughters are so beautiful, they will be married in no time," the neighbors said to Signora Bellini. "We are waiting for the wedding invitations," others said.

Signora Bellini did not trust those compliments. She told her husband, "Our nosy neighbors are giving us, *il malocchio,* the evil eye. I wish they would stop already."

The Signora had a strong belief in the power of the evil eye. This went back generations. Her mother had taught her that people were generally jealous of other's good fortune. On the surface they would shower you with compliments but in their hearts they wished you malice and bad fortune. Compliments made insincerely, and with bad intentions, could cast bad luck on the receiver. Signora Bellini worried that something could go wrong with pairing their daughters off in marriage. She made each of her daughters wear a small red charm in the shape of a horn around their necks.

The pressure for the Bellini girls to find a husband was intense. Also, it had to be in birth order. Claudia, the oldest, followed by Rosalia, then lastly Ornella, the youngest. Was love involved? Not quite. The two older girls were introduced to their prospective husbands through the recommendations of their parents.

The Bellinis made it known around town that their daughters were interested in meeting suitable prospects for marriage. They would then discreetly arrange for a mutual friend or acquaintance to approach families with sons who were agreeable to meeting their daughters.

The young men were invited over one by one to the house for a first look. Oftentimes the daughters and the prospective grooms knew each other from school or around town and had already formed an opinion of each other.

The young men arrived respectfully dressed with their hair combed and neatly greased in side parts. They met their potential wives who sat demurely on a velvet couch, with the plastic covers removed for the special occasion. The parents sat in a room off the lounge where they discreetly observed the interaction. If things seemed to be progressing well, Signor Bellini would step in to ask some questions. One of Claudia's suitors was so nervous that he spilled his orange drink on his slacks. When he answered Signor Bellini's question as to how he intended to support Claudia in the manner that she was accustomed to, he stammered so badly that his answer was unintelligible. At the end of the interrogation, he left in a puddle of sweat.

"A simple fool but a decent fellow," said Signor Bellini to his wife.

"He comes from a good family," said her mother. She turned to Claudia. "What do you think?"

Claudia shrugged. "I don't know."

"Do you not like him?" her mother asked.

"I don't know."

"Okay, that's good," said Signor Bellini. "As long as you don't hate him, we will go ahead. I will call his parents."

A year later when it was Rosalia's turn to find a husband things did not go as well. Of the boys that Signor Bellini thought suitable, *their* parents did not feel the same way. Signor Bellini was looking for a family of means but it turned out that those families did not think that a Bellini girl was good enough for their sons. However, luck was on the Bellini family's side, because the best potential match told his family that he had a soft spot for Rosalia. He knew how pretty she was, and beauty trumped common sense in these matters. Rosalia had her match, and it was a good one.

Ornella, the most beautiful of all, took the longest to find a husband. Her parents were mystified. By this time, the jewelry store was booming, and the Bellinis' finances were in good shape. Money wasn't a problem. Ornella's looks were not a problem. What was the problem?

Signor and Signora Bellini sent out their usual suitor searchers, family friends who had a knack for these things. They came back saying that they were not able to get a family to commit to a meeting.

"What is the problem?" Signor Bellini asked.

His friend rubbed his jaw as if debating whether to tell him. "Ornella is such a beautiful girl," he stammered. "She has so many boys interested in her, that she doesn't need your help."

"What kind of answer is that?" Signor Bellini boomed. "We don't need a bunch of boys – only one. Are you telling me that there isn't *one* who wants to marry her?"

The friend shrugged, unwilling to answer the question.

The years went by, and Ornella was still not married. Her parents were confused and anxious. Ornella, on the other hand, was happy. She had a full life. She worked at a high-end clothing store, she had many friends and enjoyed being independent. Her mother was furious when her neighbors and friends kept asking when an invitation was coming for Ornella's wedding.

Once again, luck was on the family's side. Giuseppe Accadi, a wealthy man in his late twenties, had had his eye on Ornella for quite some time. He came from a distinguished, prosperous family in Oristano. Ornella fell head over heels in love; it wasn't clear if it was with him or his money. Guiseppe and Ornella invited her parents to a fancy restaurant, and, over dinner, Guiseppe asked Signor Bellini for his daughter's hand in marriage.

"I need some time to think about it," Signor Bellini answered. He was more than happy to agree immediately but he didn't want Guiseppe to know that.

Signora Bellini beamed. "I am so happy for you both," she said.

Her husband kicked her under the table and shot his wife a stern look. He whispered under his breath, "Do not be so happy yet."

After dinner, they shook hands and said their *goodnights*.

"Guiseppe," I will let you know in the next few days," Signor Bellini said.

"Call me Beppe," he said, "all my friends and family do."

As they walked home, Signora Bellini asked her husband what he thought of Beppe.

"He comes from a good family, and he has a lot of money. Ornella will have the best of everything, the only thing she won't have, is his loyalty. This man will never be happy with one woman."

"Why do you say that?" his wife asked.

"I saw him eyeing the pretty waitress. I know the signs."

After marriage, each couple moved into their own home on the same street as the Bellinis. The husbands worked and the wives stayed at home. The women ran their homes just as they had learned from their mother. Every morning, after their husbands left for work, the sisters met at their mother's house for breakfast to plan their evening meals. Then they went food shopping together: to the bakery, the butcher, and the fruit and vegetable stand. Their whole day was spent planning and cooking the dinner.

Claudia wanted a baby desperately and she and her husband had been trying to conceive for some time, but nature was not co-operating.

"Someone gave you the evil eye," said Signora Bellini. "Are you wearing the evil eye necklace I gave you?"

"Please, Mother, no one gave me the evil eye," said Claudia.

"Are you following my instructions?"

"Yes," said Claudia.

Her mother advised that after 'the deed' she should lie with her legs raised up so that the *sperma* would not run out.

"How high must my legs be?" Claudia asked.

"As high as you can hold them," said her mother. "Put a cushion under your bum and lie with your legs up for at least thirty minutes."

"I already do that," said Claudia. Her eyes teared up.

"Keep in mind that on the full moon you will have a higher chance of conceiving," said her mother. "I'll let you know when it's the right day."

"Mama, that's silly," Claudia said, "that's an old wives' tale."

"It worked for me," her mother said. "Don't forget to eat figs and Roberto must wear red underpants."

"Roberto will think that I'm crazy," Claudia said without enthusiasm, "but we are willing to try anything at this point."

Three months later Claudia called her mother and her sisters to tell them that she was pregnant. She had been to her doctor to confirm it.

"Do not tell anyone yet," said her mother, firmly.

Claudia was so excited that she did not listen to her mother. She told everyone who would listen, even the man who swept the streets. Three weeks later, Claudia had cramps and was bleeding.

Her doctor ordered her on bedrest so that she wouldn't miscarry. Her mother cooked all the meals for the young couple and took care of the household chores. Claudia wasn't allowed to go to the toilet and had to use a bedpan. Despite all of the care that she took, Claudia went into labor too early, and the baby was stillborn. Claudia was inconsolable. All she could think of was that her mother had been right. *She should never have told a soul that she was pregnant. She had succumbed to the evil eye.*

Claudia's husband was transferred to Naples for his job. Claudia was heartbroken to leave her sisters and parents. She complied because her husband promised it would only be for one year. It could have been the different location, or the fact that the pressure to conceive was lessened, but whatever the reason, after the year in Naples, Claudia and her husband returned to Oristano with their long-awaited precious baby girl. Her name was Carolina. Her parents were besotted with their granddaughter. Signora Bellini was so taken with the child that she begged her two other daughters to start having babies.

Chapter Nine

A Flawed Relationship

Caroline sat on a concrete bench in the garden sipping her morning coffee. The church bells rang, and everything seemed the same as before, yet everything had changed. Caroline had felt uneasy since they arrived back from the boat trip.

Julia came out to join her and sat down.

"What a beautiful day," she said, looking up at the cloudless sky. "Are you feeling better?"

Caroline avoided eye contact. "I'm okay," she said.

"You were right," said Julia, "you shouldn't have gone swimming. You really can't swim."

"I know, I was stupid. I should have listened to my gut instinct."

"It's lucky that Antonio was able to save you."

"Yes, I was very lucky. You didn't do such a good job." Caroline looked directly at Julia.

"What do you mean?" Julia asked, her voice rising.

"You could have helped me more. You pulled your hand away when I was trying to grab it."

"You are kidding, right?" she said, flabbergasted. "Are you accusing me of deliberately not trying to help you?"

"I'm not accusing you of anything, I just think that you could have made more of an attempt."

"Wow, Caroline, I'm surprised that you should even think that. I understand that you've been through a lot, and I'm taking that into account, but I'm very hurt that you are blaming me." She got up, and walked back inside, slamming the door.

Rosalia came out with a big basket of wet laundry. She placed the basket on the grass and picked up a sheet. She lifted her arms and threw it over the clothesline then secured it with clothes pins.

Caroline jumped up. "Let me help you," she said.

"I want this to dry while the sun is shining," said Rosalia.

Caroline bent down and pulled out a towel to hang on the line. "I'm not so good at this," she said, smiling sheepishly. "I have never hung clothes out to dry on a line. We are spoiled. I use my dryer."

"We have a dryer," said Rosalia. "I prefer to use the sun as nature intended. It kills the germs and the laundry smells fresh."

"That's true," said Caroline.

"You had a bad experience yesterday on the boat," Rosalia said, "how are you feeling?"

"I am pretty shaken. It was a scary thing. I thought I was drowning. Thank God Antonio came to help me."

"Julia explained that you couldn't grab onto her outstretched hand."

Caroline put her head down, sighed deeply, and shook her head.

"What's wrong?" said Rosalia.

"Julia didn't want me to grab her hand. She pulled it away."

"What are you saying?" said Rosalia with her eyes open wide. "On purpose?"

Caroline nodded, slowly.

"You have to be mistaken," said Rosalia. "Julia is close to you and you to her. You have always been so good to her. Her mother was never around, and you took on the role of stepmother when you married Stuart."

"Life isn't easy," said Caroline. "I'm still grieving the loss of Stuart. It was so sudden. He was such a healthy, vibrant man and the heart attack was so unexpected. There were no warning signs. I still can't believe it."

"We must have faith in God, He knows what we don't. We have to trust His judgment."

"I wish I had your faith, Aunt Rosalia."

"You're shaken up. I can see the wonderful relationship you have with his daughter."

"I *was* lucky," said Caroline. "I don't know why but things have changed between Julia and I since Stuart died."

"It isn't my business," Rosalia said, "but did Stuart leave you financially comfortable?"

"Fortunately, he did, for as long as I live I have nothing to worry about," said Caroline.

"What does that mean?"

"He left me in charge of all his investments and properties and while I am living, I can use everything for my advantage. He has left instructions with his attorney. I can live at the level of comfort that we were accustomed to. I can travel, I can stay in our home, I can spend whatever I want." Caroline's forehead wrinkled. "But when I die, whatever is left, goes to his sole heir, Julia."

"I don't really understand how that works," said Rosalia. "In America things are different. Matteo just left everything to me, the money, the house, the business and he left a small portion to Adela. That way there was no confusion. This feels complicated." Rosalie sighed. "But as long as you are secure then I am happy." Rosalia sighed and looked up at Caroline. "It's so sad that your mother, my dearest sister, cannot be of help to you. She was the one who always came up with a good plan. She would sort things out between Julia and you. I try to visit her every two days. How did you find mama when you visited her?"

"Mama is a shadow of herself," said Caroline. "Physically she is there, but mentally she is gone."

"Our only hope is that she isn't in pain and suffering," said Rosalia, putting her arms around Caroline. "It's tough but we have to carry on and make the best of things."

Caroline put her head on her aunt's shoulder. They walked arm in arm back into the house.

As they entered, Caroline heard Julia talking on the phone.

"Can you believe that she accused me of almost letting her drown?"

As soon as she saw Caroline, she abruptly ended the call.

"Who were you talking to?" asked Caroline.

"James."

"Were you talking about me?"

"No, Caroline I was not talking about you. Don't be so paranoid," Julia said, exasperated. She turned to Adela and Luca who were sitting on the sofa scrolling through their phones. "Was I talking about Caroline?" she asked them.

"We weren't paying attention to your conversation," Luca said, and Adela nodded in agreement.

"Mama we are going to town to get ice-cream," Adela said, "do you want to come with us?"

"No, thank you," said Rosalia. "I'm going to start the dinner soon. Have fun."

Adela turned to Julia, "Would you like to come?"

"Okay," she said.

"I just have to freshen up," said Adela. "I won't be long."

"I'll meet you all at the gelateria. I need a walk, so I'll leave now," said Julia, heading for the door.

"Do you know where the ice cream place is?" Luca asked.

"I'll find it. What's the name? I'll use my GPS."

"It's a little complicated to get to Piazza Europa," Luca said.

"I'm a city girl, I know how to find places," Julia answered, and she walked out of the door.

"She is so impatient," Adela said to Luca. "This isn't a race. We are taking a stroll into town."

When they got to the gelateria, Adela couldn't see Julia; she was nowhere in sight.

"I knew this was going to happen," Adela said to Luca. "The piazza is not easy to find."

They waited ten minutes then went inside. The colorful mounds of ice cream and gelato mixed with ripe fruit was like something out of a fairy tale. Adela and Luca knew exactly what they wanted. Adela asked for Stracciatella, vanilla with chocolate shavings. Luca preferred coffee ice cream. Both chose cups instead of sugared cones.

They made their way outside and sat on a bench in the shade waiting for Julia. After they had finished eating their ice cream, Luca texted Julia: *"Where are you?"*

"I'm just across the street from you. I'm having a coffee. I can see you both sitting on the bench."

"We have been waiting for you. Come on over, what flavor ice cream do you want?"

"I'm coming in a minute. I don't want ice cream, thanks. It's too fattening."

"Madon! Damn!" Luca said to Adela. "She is so inconsiderate. She is having a coffee right opposite here, while we are waiting and worrying about her."

Adela rolled her eyes and shook her head.

When Julia finally joined them, she didn't sit down. "I want to go clothes shopping," she said. "Where are the best clothing stores in town?"

"We like Fashionista Boutique," said Adela. "My mother buys all her clothes from there, in fact the last time Caroline was visiting, she bought a whole bunch of things there too."

"Oh, well then, that's not the place for me." Julia smirked. "I wouldn't call Caroline a fashion plate."

"She always looks elegant," said Adela.

"Are you not close to your stepmother?" asked Luca.

"No." Her jaw tightened. "We are on courteous terms."

"What does that mean?" Luca looked at his wife.

"Termini cortesi," she answered.

"Aah," Luca said. "I thought the two of you had a good relationship."

"Caroline is two-faced," Julia said. "That's my take on her."

"I'm surprised you say that," said Adela. "What do you mean?"

"Fake. She's fake."

"How so?" Adela was visibly shaken.

"After my dad died, she became greedy and took all his money."

"Wasn't there a will?" asked Adela.

"There was. Her interpretation wasn't fair."

"Surely everything is legal?" said Luca.

"Put it this way. I got nothing, zip, zero. But in the far future when she dies, then I get what is left."

"That seems fair," Adela said.

Luca nodded in agreement.

"She's a very healthy woman, and it could take years. She could live until she is one hundred."

"We hope she will," Adela said. "You and your husband live a very nice life, so I wouldn't worry about it."

Julia changed the subject. "It doesn't look like this town has any big label clothing stores," she said. "Maybe I'll go and get my nails done." She held up her hands and examined her fingers turning them this way and that. "The next time I come to Italy, I'll bring my husband with. We will go to Rome and Milan. That will be more our style."

Chapter Ten

Tomato Sauce Day

Caroline woke up, before the sun rose, to get ready to help the family make fresh tomato sauce to last the year. This was an annual tradition that Rosalia practiced since she was a young girl. Most of the meals that she cooked daily contained the tomato sauce from the rows of jars that were stored in the basement. Store bought sauce wasn't even a consideration in the house; that was akin to a cardinal sin.

Salvatore played an important role in the tomato canning process. It was he who had cultivated and grown the rows of tomato plants in the garden. The day before the big event, he would transport mounds of red plum tomatoes in a wheelbarrow to the back porch.

Luca rose very early to sterilize the jars and lay them out in rows on the long wooden table. Adela and Salvatore dropped the tomatoes into huge vats of boiling water that bubbled over an open flame. Rosalia stirred the thick red sauce with a large wooden paddle in wide circular motions

"How can I help?" asked Caroline. She was glad that the canvas canopy offered shade in the sweltering heat of the sun.

"There will be plenty to do after the tomatoes have boiled. I will need your help filling the jars."

Julia popped her head around the door. "Wow, this is major work," she said, "can't you just buy tomato sauce at the store?"

Adela shot her a look. "It may be a lot of work, but it's worth it. Can you please help me chop the garlic?"

"I'm sorry, I don't want to ruin my nails, I just had them done. I am going into town to do some gift shopping. I'll see you all later."

Salvatore poured the steaming tomatoes into giant colanders to drain and cool, then he transferred batches into an electric food mill to crush and puree the tomatoes into a thick velvet sauce. Beads of sweat dotted his forehead and ran down his face.

"This brings back such good memories of my childhood," said Caroline. "Aunt Rosalia, do you remember us spilling the sauce all over the floor? "

"Yes! That was the time that we wasted so much sauce because we dropped the vat." She laughed.

The family felt a sense of accomplishment after the rows of glass jars with basil leaves were filled and sealed. Rosalia had made fresh pasta earlier in the day, so that they could enjoy the fruits of their labor. Nothing tasted as good as pasta with homemade tomato sauce.

Salvatore took a mouthful and gestured with his fingers in a circle that it was perfect. He wiped his mouth with a napkin. "You will all have to excuse me, but I have a dentist appointment this afternoon."

Rosalia looked at him er with concern. "What a pity," she said, "you must be tired. I know I am."

"I will be fine," he said, "I just have to sit in the dentist chair while he cleans my teeth. I will have an early night tonight."

Salvatore left the dentist's office and as he stepped out the door of the building onto Piazza Eleanore, he saw Julia walking briskly to the edge of the square. At first, he wasn't sure because the sun was in his eyes, but then he moved into the shade, and he couldn't mistake her. She was wearing a bright orange dress and a white straw sunhat, her long blonde hair tumbling over her shoulders. Julia stood out like a sunflower in a barren wheat field. She strode with purpose and Salvatore wondered where she was going in such a hurry. He decided to investigate. He upped his pace and followed her. He walked under the eaves close to the storefronts, so as not to be noticed. When Salvatore came closer to Julia, he slowed down and kept a few paces behind. She was focused on a conversation on her phone and was not paying attention to anyone around her. She turned down a side street, picking up her stride along the cobbled lane. She stopped in front of a small hotel. Salvatore was familiar with most of the hotels in the town but had never seen this one. It was hidden in an alley between the larger buildings. From a distance he couldn't read the name of the hotel on the small brass plaque on the wall.

Julia walked up the steps to the entrance and nodded to the doorman. Then she walked through the polished wooden doors. Salvatore waited for a while before moving closer to look at the plaque—Casa Castello. He rubbed his jaw and bit his bottom lip. He shook his head and pondered. *What was Julia up to? Who was she visiting in this hotel?* Before the doorman could ask him any questions, he turned around and headed back home.

He arrived back home just in time for dinner. Rosalia jumped up and handed him a bowl of *pasta fagioli.*

"How was the dentist?" Rosalia asked.

"It went okay. I never like going there," he said, "but it has to be done."

As soon as he sat down, he could tell that Luca and Adela were in a bad mood. They often argued, so Salvatore was not too concerned. "Why the long faces?" he asked the young couple.

"Luca had a Zoom meeting with his boss today," said Adela. "He was supposed to ask for a raise. As per usual he did not." She sighed dramatically.

"It wasn't the right time," Luca snapped at her.

"It's never the right time but you have to be firm and not back down," she seethed. "You work like a dog at the trucking company, and they don't appreciate you. They were happy to promote you but not to pay you properly for the new responsibilities."

Luca's face flushed scarlet. "I wish you would stop nagging me. I didn't have the opportunity," he said, "I tried speaking to him, but he interrupted me by pointing out the things that I could do better."

"You should have spoken up," she said. "You will never get a raise, if you don't open your mouth."

Salvatore quicky intervened, he could tell that the argument was escalating. "It's not easy to ask for something when the other person is not open to listening," he said.

Caroline added, "It's not fair when you feel that you aren't compensated for a job well done."

Chapter Eleven

The Golden Child

Julia had been the perfect child in her parents' eyes. They doted on her so much that they made the decision not to have any more children. "How can any other child be better than her?" they said to one another. She was way ahead of her milestones—she held her head up as soon as she was born. They marveled at the way she raised her body and looked out of the bassinet in the delivery room to observe surroundings. She walked at nine months, and she spoke full sentences at a year and two months. Her parents, Jill and Stuart, were so proud of their baby girl. They gloated about how they had produced such a perfect child. Stuart and Jill felt sorry for their friends' children who were not as advanced. When a parent at the private pre-school where Julia attended boasted about their child's progress, they shot each other an all-knowing look—their child far surpassed that! Jill diligently sought out only 'gifted' playmates for playdates. They enrolled Julia in a superior academic kindergarten in another town and hired a driver to drive her there and back.

Two events happened simultaneously that changed the trajectory of Julia's *perfect life*.

The first event was that when seven-year-old Julia hit the second grade, a gradual realization dawned upon the young girl that she wasn't so special after all. The cruel trick that her parents had played on her by making her feel so exceptional came crashing down when she could not master the class curriculum. Where some of her peers understood the math concepts, she did not. When others were already reading fluently, she had a problem untangling the letters. Julia was tested for learning disabilities and the results showed that she was dyslexic. The school recommended that she should repeat her grade. Her mother was so furious that she moved her daughter to another school.

The second knock that ended her secure life was when she turned ten. Her mother ran off with the tennis coach and left her behind with her father.

She realized right away that if she was so special then why would her mother abandon her?

Stuart tried to explain the circumstances to his bereft daughter. "Mom went to live with Joe. She wasn't happy here anymore."

"She doesn't love us anymore?" asked Julia, with tears rolling down her cheeks.

"Mommy will always love you. It's me she doesn't love," he explained.

Julia's grades started slipping and she hated going to school. She was no longer the popular girl who everyone wanted to be friends with. Her father was busy at the law firm and by the time he came home, she was asleep. Julia had a nanny to take care of her. The nanny soon recognized that her ward was overindulged and spoiled. Julia had never been told 'no' and now when she was admonished for bad behavior, it led to many hours of screaming and crying. Her nanny did not put up with tantrums, and Julia was given 'time out' and closed in the small office at the back of the house. She lay on the floor and wept until she apologized for her bad behavior.

Julia missed her mother. In the beginning she cried for her every day. But later she accepted the situation. She built her mother into a paragon of virtue. She understood that she was unlovable and that was the reason her mother had left her behind. The only contact Julia had with her mother were the birthday cards that she sent. Julia treasured the cards, keeping them safe in a red velvet heart-shaped box.

Just as Julia was adapting to life alone with her father, he brought home a woman.

"This is daddy's special friend, Caroline," he said. "She is going to be a big part of our family." He put his arm around the woman and drew her closer to him. "You know how sad Daddy has been?" He said while reaching for

Julia's hand, "Caroline makes me very happy, and I know that she will make you happy too."

Julia deduced that her mother had left because she wasn't happy. Then her father had met someone who made him happy. "You don't know what makes me happy!" she screamed and threw her tablet onto the tiled floor smashing it into pieces. Julia ran to her room and slammed the door. She pushed her desk against the door and sat on her bed and cried.

"Open the door this minute," yelled her father. "She's being a brat," her father said to Caroline. "I'm sorry, she's not usually like this."

"Let her be," said Caroline, "it's understandable that she is upset."

Caroline slowly won over Julia by not forcing the relationship. Julia said some hurtful things to Caroline, but Caroline let it slide. She did not tattle-tale to her husband about his daughter's rude behavior. She slowly won over the girl's trust.

Caroline overheard Julia tell her father that Caroline looked like a giraffe and wasn't as pretty as her mother. It stung, but Caroline didn't say anything. What hurt her most was that Stuart didn't contradict his daughter's nasty comments.

"I think she sucks," Julia added pouring more salt on Caroline's wounds.

"You don't have to worry, sweetie," said her father, "you will always be the number one girl in my life."

When Julia was older, and started dating, her choices of partners were substandard. She was drawn to men who were emotionally unavailable. Julia was not attracted to the boys who liked her. She wanted the ones who weren't interested in her and were a challenge to pursue. Julia was a pretty girl, a forceful girl with definite opinions. That would be acceptable if she was open to other opinions, but she wasn't, she had to be right and everyone else was wrong. She never lacked male attention because of her physical attributes but once the novelty wore off, her looks didn't compensate for her character.

Her father became concerned.

"I don't understand why the guys all drop her," Stuart said to his wife.

"Julia is an independent woman," said Caroline, "and some men are intimidated by that."

"Well, we will have to find her a 'real' man who wants an independent thinker, not a Barbie doll."

Opportunity comes for those who seek it and soon enough a young and upcoming lawyer, James Callahan, was seated for a job interview opposite Stuart. Stuart, the sole operating owner of his law firm, Anderson and Associates LLP, liked to interview potential applicants for himself. Unbeknownst to James, who presumed there would be many applicants for the position, he was a shoe-in. Stuart had already made up his mind to hire him. Stuart was a good judge of character, and he liked what he saw in James. James had a stellar resume; he had graduated from a top law school with honors. He showed drive and ambition.

He was tall and good-looking, and the most important qualification of all was that James Callahan was single.

"Would you be willing to relocate to Miami from Boston?" Stuart asked.

"Yes, no problem," James replied.

"We have some excellent private schools in the area if you have children," he said.

"I don't have any," said James.

"There are many job opportunities here for a spouse," said James.

"I'm not married," said James.

That closed the deal.

"I'll let you know in the next few days. It was good meeting you," said Stuart, standing up and shaking his hand firmly. In his mind's eye he was already concocting a plan to introduce James to his daughter.

James was hired at the salary that he had asked for. Stuart made sure the negotiations led to an offer that James could not refuse. As soon as James was ensconced in a large corner office facing the expansive bay, Stuart invited him out for a congratulatory dinner.

"I'll take you to the best steakhouse in Miami," he said.

"That would be great," said James, "as long as they have a fish choice. I am pescatarian."

Bourbon Steak was bustling on a Friday night when Stuart and James were led to the table by an elegant hostess. Stuart, a regular diner, knew the maître'd well and they were seated at the best table in the house.

"Cool place," said James. "Thanks for inviting me."

"The food is to die for," said Stuart. He rubbed his hands together. "By the way," he said, "I have invited my wife and daughter to join us. They should be here jointly."

"That's great," James said. He was a little taken aback.

As soon as they were seated, the waiter brought a basket of bread and complimentary fries with dipping sauces to the table. They each ordered a cocktail.

Two stunning women descended the staircase and Stuart immediately stood up and waved. "There they are!" he exclaimed. He turned to James. "That's my wife and my daughter."

Both men stood up to greet them.

Heads turned as the women approached the table. Both were blonde but that is where the similarity ended. Tall and slender, with her hair cut in a bob and dressed in a body fitting couture dress, the older one looked as if she stepped off the cover of *Vogue*. The shorter woman was petite with waist-length hair, wearing a black jumpsuit, and impossibly high stiletto heels. Both women were beautiful. Stuart kissed each one on the cheek.

"James, this is my wife, Caroline and our daughter, Julia," Stuart said, beaming with pride.

James shook both their hands. His eyes scanned the tall, blonde woman and the petite younger woman with the dazzling smile. A server pulled out a chair for each woman to be seated.

"James has just joined our company, and this is a celebratory dinner," said Stuart.

Julia had already been prepped about James a few days prior. Her father was impressed with his credentials. A Harvard Law graduate and had interned at a prestigious law firm. He arrived with stellar recommendations, all the potential for a suitable associate and match for his daughter. Julia's dating record had not been extraordinary; she was attracted to 'bad boys' and they didn't make good partners.

The trajectory of all her relationships followed the same pattern. At the start everything was hunky-dory. She was the perfect arm candy for a shallow partner but as soon as her true nature came out and her faults were exposed, the goodbye speech was always the same. *"It's not you, it's me,"* they said, making a quick exit. Julia blamed everyone else for the demise of the relationship. "He was so selfish, and self-absorbed, bordering on mental abuse," she told her father. Stuart decided to take matters in his own hands to sort the chaff from the wheat. He thought that James was the perfect match for his daughter. The dinner ended successfully; James appeared taken with Julia.

At the office, the following day, James asked Stuart if it would be okay for him to call Julia and ask her out. Stuart replied that he needed time to think it through.

"I'll let Stuart stew," he said to Caroline with a wink after he got home. "He must never know how keen I am."

After two weeks, Stuart gave James the go ahead to ask Julia out.

"Do not mess this up," Stuart told his daughter. "You have to play your cards right. No whining and acting like a diva."

"Come on, Dad, I'm not that bad," she said.

"You are that bad," he said. "If things work out between the two of you, then I can think about him becoming a partner in the future."

"This isn't the 1900s Dad. You don't have to 'arrange' a marriage for me."

"I'm just giving you a little nudge," Stuart said. "It's time you settled down and started a family."

Julia smiled to herself because she had been contemplating the same thing. "I'll try my best," she said.

Chapter Twelve

Costa Smeralda

Caroline, Julia, Rosalia and Salvatore were in the Costa Smeralda. The older couple had taken Caroline and Julia for a few days sojourn to their favorite beachside resort.

"It's a beautiful part of northern Sardinia where the *persone alla moda,* the fashionable people, are," said Salvatore in the car on the way there.

"Where the cool people hang out," Caroline explained.

"Julia, trust me, you will like it," Salvatore added. "There are magnificent beaches and great restaurants."

"And the best shopping," Caroline added.

Beppe and Ornella's yacht was docked close to the resort where the family was staying.

After they unpacked and rested for a while, they headed out for dinner in the resort at the popular seafood restaurant on the water. A live band played music, and most diners were in a dancing mood. Salvatore pulled Rosalia up to dance. They moved with joyful abandon and Salvatore sang along with the singer in the band.

Julia was wearing a long white backless dress that looked as if she had been poured into it. Her streaked blonde hair was twisted into a messy topknot, and she had tucked a red hibiscus flower behind her ear. The men were not shy to show their admiration for her while their wives looked annoyed. Julia was used to male attention; she laughed, shrugged, and threw her hands up in the air. She always enjoyed being the focal point.

After dinner, everyone retired to their rooms. It wasn't long before Caroline woke up feeling ill. She had stomach cramps, and the room was spinning. She barely got to the bathroom in time to throw up into the toilet. Caroline crawled back to the bedroom but was too weak to climb back onto her bed. She lay sprawled out on the cold marble floor. Caroline reached for her phone on the side table and tried to grab it, but it fell onto the floor under the bed, and she was too weak to retrieve it. She knew that Julia was in the adjoining suite, but she didn't have the strength to call out.

She lay in the fetal position, her hair matted from vomit, praying for daylight when someone would come and find her.

Finally, she called out to Julia. Her voice came out in a hoarse whisper. She reached for a slipper next to her, picked it up and banged it on the common wall.

Julia came running into the room. "Caroline, what happened?" she said, shocked to find her stepmother lying on the floor. "Did you fall?"

Julia tried to lift Caroline, but she was too heavy.

"Call the front desk," Caroline whimpered.

"Oh right," said Julia. "Where is the front desk button?" she said panicking. "Did you eat the oysters?" she asked. "I bet it's the oysters."

Two security men entered the suite and lifted Caroline onto the bed.

"I think we should call for medical assistance," said one of them. "There is an ambulance service in Porto Cervo, and they will transport her to the closest hospital in Olbia.

"I don't want to go to the hospital. Please," Caroline begged, "I'm feeling a bit better."

"Let the paramedics come and check you out," said Julia. "Let them make that assessment that you are okay." She turned to the men. "How far is Olbia from here?"

"About a forty-minute drive," one man said.

Julia immediately called Rosalia. "Where are you?" she asked, her voice rising.

"At the pool," said Rosalia, "What is the matter?"

"I found Caroline lying on the floor in her room. She had thrown up all over the place. I called the front desk, and they sent up security. They want to call for an ambulance to transport her to the hospital in Olbia.

"Oh no!" gasped Rosalia. "Was it something she ate?"

"Probably the oysters from last night," said Julia.

"I'm coming up now," said Rosalia. She explained the situation to Salvatore and they both rushed in their wet bathing suits to Caroline's room. They found Caroline in bed, pale and weak.

"Did you have diarrhea?" they asked.

"Just terrible cramps," she said.

"What are those bright yellow smudges on your lips?" Rosalia asked.

"That was the color of my vomit," Caroline said. "It was fluorescent."

"That's bile," said Julia. "I know from when I've been sick."

"I think we should we call the paramedics?" said Rosalia.

"The hospital is a forty-minute drive from here," said Caroline. "I really don't want to go. Let me rest and I'm sure I will feel better later."

"Okay, let's wait a while," said Rosalia, "I will sit with you. Try and sleep, that will do you good. I think you must have eaten something bad."

As soon as Caroline fell asleep, Salvatore and Julia left the room. Rosalia sat crocheting a doily for the back of her sofa, she never sat idle. Soon, she was sleeping too, her glasses slipping off her nose as she snored lightly.

Caroline woke up needing to pee. She stood unsteadily and held onto the wall, inching her way to the bathroom. She saw that the toilet was clogged with vomit and tissues. Caroline decided to use Julia's bathroom instead. She tapped lightly on the adjoining door and there was no answer. Julia must have still been at lunch. Caroline went into the bathroom and as she sat down on the toilet, she noticed Julia's leopard skin cosmetic case gaping open. There was a plastic bottle of fluorescent bright yellow liquid visible in the case. The label said: *Anti-Freeze Coolant. This is the evidence that Julia is trying to poison me.* She knew that she had to get her phone and take a screenshot of what she found. Caroline mustered up all her energy to go back to her room and get her phone. She went back into Julia's bathroom and took a photo of the coolant.

She heard the suite door click open, and she quickly flushed the toilet.

"Who is there?" Julia called out.

"It's only me," she said. Her heart was pounding. "I had to use your toilet. Mine is clogged."

"You gave me such a shock," said Julia. "The door was unlocked?"

"Thankfully, yes," said Caroline.

"You should have texted me, I nearly died of fright." Julia put her head in her hands and exhaled deeply.

"Sorry, but who else could it be?"

"You never know. I'm a woman alone and things happen."

Julia peeked through the bathroom door and her eyes went to the make-up bag. She flung open the door and grabbed her make-up bag. She immediately pulled out the yellow container. "What is this?" she said.

"I don't know," said Caroline, "you tell me."

"It says anti-freeze. Why would this be in my cosmetic bag? Who put it in there?"

"Someone who wants to poison someone," said Caroline, wincing.

"That's crazy." Julia twirled her pointer finger towards her forehead: the universal sign of crazy. "You are crazy. Why would I have coolant in my bag? I don't even have a car?"

"You tell me." Caroline clenched her jaw. "Things are very weird, I don't know what I've ever done to you, but things are not adding up."

"What are you talking about?" Julia's eyes widened with indignation. "First you insinuate that I wanted to drown you and now this. Caroline, I really think that something is wrong with you. You are paranoid." Julia paced up and down. She shook her head. "I think that you should speak to someone. When we get back to the US you should see a psychiatrist."

Caroline went back to her room, shaken.

Rosalia opened her eyes, "I must have fallen asleep," she said.

Caroline sat on the edge of her bed.

"How are you feeling?" Rosalia asked.

"Better," she said, her voice hoarse. Caroline did not divulge her suspicions; she knew that they sounded crazy. No one would believe her. But she did have a screenshot of Julia's cosmetic bag with the anti-freeze coolant inside.

Chapter Thirteen

Tension Mounts in Cagliari

Caroline was quiet as Salvatore drove the family to Cagliari, in his minivan. He and Rosalia looked forward to showing Julia the capital of Sardinia, a beautiful, bustling city with restaurants and shopping. No one would have guessed the tension between Caroline and Julia. Caroline had recovered and there was an unspoken truce. Only Caroline knew that she had accused Julia of trying to kill her; that was not conducive to having a pleasant outing.

As they drove closer to the city, the medieval hilltop town of Castello loomed over them. Salvatore was familiar with the town and could have found his way blindfolded. He parked the van close to Via Roma where many of the fashion boutiques were.

"I can get everything I want and more in Miami," Julia said, "but it would be nice to bring back a few outfits directly from Italy."

Rosalia, Salvatore and Caroline preferred not to shop but to have a coffee in the square instead.

"I'm not a shopper," Caroline said. "I can get everything online."

"The problem with that is you never know how things will fit," said Rosalia. "Besides I like to feel the fabrics in my hand."

"That's true," Caroline agreed. "Most of my clothes don't fit and then I'm too lazy to send them back." She laughed. "Look at this blouse I'm wearing, it's about two sizes too big."

"I have a lot of my outfits custom made," said Rosalia. She stroked the fabric of her skirt. "I have an excellent seamstress whom I've used for years. I choose the fabric, and she does the rest."

"That is wonderful," Caroline said.

Just then the waitress approached to take their order. Three espressos and a tiramisu to share.

"I'm fortunate that Ornella and Beppe have fabric stores, I choose whatever I want and put it on my account. Of course, I never pay." She laughed.

"I have worn the same clothes for twenty years," Salvatore said. "What do I need? A few shirts and some pants. It's only since we got married that Rosalia insists that I dress better," he said, "she now is the commandant of my wardrobe."

"Julia is a shopaholic," said Caroline. "She is fortunate that she can afford to buy whatever she wants." She drummed her fingers on the table.

"That's lucky. Her husband must be a generous man," said Rosalia. "He seems very caring – he calls her all the time."

"He is both generous and caring," said Caroline. She bit her lip debating whether to tell them that he was in fact in town. She decided not to. Julia would just deny the conversation that Caroline overheard.

"Is she wealthy in her own right?" asked Salvatore.

"She will be one day," Caroline said. "Stuart left his estate to me and after I pass on, she will get everything."

"Nothing now?' he asked.

"Nothing now, except their house," said Caroline. "Julia is not happy." She lowered her head and sighed. "Long before Stuart passed away, we discussed his will and I asked him to please see that when he died, God forbid, to please leave his daughter financially comfortable. His feelings were that she would spend her inheritance in no time. So, he set it up that I would live off the estate and what was left, she would get. I wanted him to change that. I didn't want her to resent me. No one expected him to die so young. It was a great shock."

"Well, she has a great life. Her husband makes a good salary so she can't complain," said Salvatore.

"Money is a terrible divider," said Caroline. "I keep getting the feeling that Julia can't wait for me to die."

"That's terrible!" Rosalia said. "Don't even think that way. You live your life to the fullest." She took a sip of coffee. "I was lucky Matteo left me very secure. I am very appreciative."

"Every woman or man should have their own money that they earned themselves," said Caroline. "Unfortunately, my generation was not taught that. One should never have to rely on anyone for their existence. I wish my parents told me that."

"You are right," said Rosalia. "My sisters and I were raised to marry well, and our job was to raise a family and make it possible for our husbands to go out and earn a living for us. That was the old-fashioned way."

Julia walked towards them balancing shopping bags in each hand.

"You were successful, I see," said Salvatore. "Sit under the umbrella with us and have a cold drink."

"I found some nice things." She smiled. "Also, some great jeans and polo shirts for James."

"Mission accomplished," said Salvatore.

"We need to go to the Mercato di San Benadetto to pick up vegetables and seafood," said Rosalia. "Did you bring the cooler bags?" she asked her husband.

"Of course," he said. "We never go to Cagliari without bringing back fish."

Julia bit her lower lip in frustration and asked the waiter for more ice with her soda. "I don't understand why Italians are so stingy with their ice. They bring a glass of Coke with one block of ice, it's ridiculous."

"Have something to eat," coaxed Salvatore, "then we can go to the market. It's indoors so it's nice and cool."

"I'm exhausted," said Julia, "and my feet are killing me, can we please go back home? I don't want to walk around a market."

"We will be quick," said Rosalia. "You can sit in the shade and wait for us."

"I would still like to look around," Caroline said, "I was here a few years back, but I would like to refresh my memory."

Julia frowned. "It's always about you, Caroline," she said, raising her voice, "I'm exhausted and all you think about is doing what you want to do."

"We came all this way," Rosalia said. "Let's just walk around a bit, then go to the market and then we will drive back."

"Can I get a taxi back to Oristano?" Julia asked.

"It's too far for a taxi but you can take the train," said Salvatore. "We can drop you off at the station. You will probably be back in Oristano at the same time as us."

Julia abruptly stood up and threw her drink onto the table—soda and ice splashed over the red and white tablecloth. The other diners looked up in shock.

"You know what?" she yelled. "I've had enough of this place. Everything just sucks! I wish I had never come."

"Calm down, you are making a scene," Caroline whispered.

"I don't care if I'm making a scene. No one knows what crap I have to put up with from you," she shouted at Caroline.

"Okay, okay," said Rosalia jumping up. "We will go home. It's okay." She gestured to Salvatore to pay the check. They quickly gathered their things and hurriedly made their way back to the van. Julia stormed off cursing under her breath.

Chapter Fourteen

James and Julia's Wedding

James and Julia's wedding had been the social event of the year in Miami. Julia had fantasized about her wedding from childhood. She sketched pages of wedding dresses since her teens. Some were princess-like and puffy with white and net fabric billowing out. The figure she drew was always very tall and thin, with an oval face and a long neck, and long arms and legs. The hair was styled either up in a bun or cascading across skinny shoulders. In some of her drawings, she added a long veil. Other versions had a tight-fitting bodice with a body-skimming skirt ending in a fish tail. The shoes were always pointed with stiletto heels as high as her imagination allowed and impossible to walk in in the real world.

Her bouquets were variations of flowers and greenery. Intricate flowers such as roses and lilies were too difficult for her to draw so she stuck to simple flowers, tulips and daisies. Julia filled pages with renderings of her engagement ring fantasies. The diamond was always very large. Sometimes it was a perfectly round or oval solitaire, other times it was circled with smaller diamonds. Her very favorite diamond type was the Asscher Cut; she had seen it in a wedding magazine and cut out the picture to pin on her vision board. It was a square cut with a trillion facets that allowed the light to play in a mesmerizing way.

Her dream diamond wish came to a halt when her father got engaged to Caroline and gave her an Asscher Cut diamond ring. When Julia saw it, she ran to her room, shut the door, and burst out crying. She took a Sharpie and scribbled over the picture of her favorite ring on her vision board while tears splashed down her face.

Years later, when James proposed to her on an air balloon floating above the South of France, he presented her with the ring that they had designed with a jeweler — a huge rectangular emerald cut diamond showcasing its clarity and transparency. The ring was prettier than any she could have dreamed of. Julia's heart was filled with joy.

Her wedding dress chose her, it knocked her pre-conceived ideas out of her head. She was attending an Elie Saab fashion show in Milan when the most beautiful bridal dress she could ever have imagined came down the runway on a model. It was neither voluminous nor figure-hugging as she had sketched all those years ago. It was simple and stark, white, and draped like a Grecian robe. It was like nothing that she had ever seen before, and she knew that she had to have it. And she did.

A wedding planner did all the grunt work. Julia conjured up her desires, and they magically appeared. James had little say in the preparations of his wedding, but he preferred it that way. Whatever his fiancée wished for was fine with him. Her father, Stuart, had one directive only, *whatever her heart desired was fine with him.* Caroline had no say in the choice of dress that she was to wear. Julia explained that it was her wedding, therefore it was her decision what her stepmother would wear. It was a long, gray, sparkly dress that was perfectly appropriate for blending into the background. The bridesmaids were chosen for their looks. Only attractive, slender, and well-groomed women were selected even if they hardly knew the bride. However, there was one caveat, they were instructed not to upstage the bride. Julia's closest friend was short and chubby, so she was excluded. The bridesmaid dresses were couture in a subtle shade of taupe.

There was great excitement when Julia's mother, who had run off with the tennis coach and had been missing from her daughter's entire life, had now declared that she would be attending her daughter's special day. Against her father's wishes, Julia insisted on sending her mother an invitation. Julia never dared tell *her* what to wear, she didn't want to jinx the miracle. She also asked her mother if she would do her the greatest honor by walking her down the aisle together with her father. Her mother agreed as long as all the flight and hotel expenses would be covered for her and her current boyfriend. She insisted on first class air and an hotel suite.

The wedding took place at Vizcaya, a historic Italian Renaissance-style estate located in Miami. The ceremony was in the magnificent gardens overlooking the bay. The party planner and his team created a spectacular reception with food, drinks and music that the guests still talked about. The guests also still talked about another aspect of the spectacular event. After the dinner was served and before the guests were called to the Viennese table for dessert, a drunk Julia took the microphone onto the dance floor and announced, "would you please all leave and go home? I've had enough."

Chapter Fifteen

Suspicious Behavior

After breakfast, Salvatore watched as Julia was getting ready to go into town. She was gathering her phone and her purse. She paused and checked herself out in the mirror above the mantel.

"I'm going to run some errands," she announced. "I need to get out and walk. It clears my head."

Salvatore waited for her to leave and then he left out the back door to follow her. Julia walked briskly and he made sure to keep a few feet behind. He wore sunglasses and a large sunhat and walked with his head down. Julia was an easy target; she was distracted by filming herself on her phone while giving a running commentary. She almost walked into a pillar and tripped off the side of the sidewalk. She regained her balance, dusted herself off, and carried on filming.

Julia had a travel blog on Instagram with thousands of followers, her goal was to reach a million and it irked her that numbers were not rising. James joked that the cost of their trips that he paid for were a very expensive ego boost, and the money she earned from promotions was hardly enough for one expensive meal.

Salvatore wanted to get to the bottom of where Julia was sneaking off to in an unfamiliar city. She stopped at the same small hotel as before, nodded to the doorman and walked up the few steps to the entrance. Salvatore sat at a table on the sidewalk of a small bar across the street. He ordered an espresso and waited. After an hour Julia came back out the door, but she was not alone. She was with a woman. A young woman, with pink hair and tattoos down both arms. Salvatore's mouth fell open. He recognized the girl right away; her name was Pia, and she was a good friend of Rosalia's daughter, Adela. *What was she doing with Julia?* Salvatore didn't think that they even knew each other. The two women smiled and chatted, linking arms as they crossed the street and walked towards the café. Salvatore got up, grabbed a complimentary newspaper from the café and moved to a table against the wall.

"Is this good for you?" Julia asked Pia, pointing to an empty two-seat table a few rows in front of Salvatore. Pia nodded and they sat down. Julia gestured to the waiter, "Two cappuccinos per favore?" she said.

The waiter looked at his watch. He looked perplexed.

"What's wrong?" Julia asked Pia. "Did I say it incorrectly?"

"It's after twelve noon and we don't order cappuccinos at this time of day. Only for breakfast."

"That's crazy," Julia said. "I want one and I'm the customer, so I am always right." She turned to the waiter. "One cappuccino please and a piece of ricotta cake."

"I will have an espresso and a tiramisu," Pia added.

Julia pulled her chair closer to Pia and leaned in. "I am so happy that you have agreed to do this."

"I gave it a lot of thought," Pia replied. "I am very close to Luca and Adela, and to be honest, if they thought it was a bad idea, I wouldn't do this. They explained the circumstances and it makes sense to me."

"I know it sounds crazy, but it's a win-win situation for both of us," said Julia. "I get what I want, and you get financial compensation. As you said, you are struggling to make a living as a hairdresser, and this will give you financial security."

Salvatore's hands shook so badly that he could hardly hold the newspaper. He couldn't believe what he was hearing. When he saw the women pay their bill and get ready to leave, he quietly stood up and walked inside the café. He watched as Pia hugged Julia. She left first and then Julia took a compact mirror out of her bag and re-applied her lipstick.

Salvatore strode out of the café and acted surprised to see Julia sitting there. He waved.

"Fancy meeting you here!" she exclaimed, smiling. She ran her fingers through her hair and lifted her sunglasses onto her head.

"I was in town and just came in to grab a cup of coffee," he said, nonchalantly. "Are you having lunch?"

"I just finished," she said. "I went for a facial. I desperately needed one, so I googled and found this spa over there." She pointed to the building where she had just come from.

Her face was perfectly made up and although Salvatore did not know much about facials, he did know that when Rosalia returned from having one, her skin was makeup free and glowing. He also knew that a small boutique hotel would not have a spa.

"You really find your way around," he said. "It's impressive."

"I'm a seasoned traveler." She laughed, then flashed a nervous smile. "I make myself at home in any city."

"I'm pleased to see that you are having a good time with us. It's been a pleasure to have you as our guest." He chewed the bottom of his lip. "Anyone connected to Caroline is always welcome in our home. She is very special to my wife. We adore her and will do anything for her."

Julia kept very quiet.

"Is there a problem with you and Caroline," Salvatore asked. "I seem to feel some tension."

"You are very preceptive," Julia said. "Caroline is not the sweet, kind person that everyone thinks. She has a very mean side that only I seem to see."

"I disagree with you," said Salvatore. "Rosalia has known her since she was a child, and she has always been a good, kind and caring woman. The family also knows how good she has been to you since you were little. Do you agree?"

Julia shrugged, seemingly unwilling to answer the question.

"Why are you so rude to her?" said Salvatore. "It's really not nice."

"She's a bitch, that's why," said Julia. Her voice seethed with anger.

Salvatore bent his head and looked Julia straight in the eye. "Do not even think of harming Caroline. Do you understand? We take family very seriously here and if you do anything to Caroline, you will be very sorry."

Julia paled. She tilted her head back to look up to him. "I hope you are not threatening me," she said. "You may have your way of doing things over here, but fortunately I live in the real world, and I don't have to put up with you or your family's crap."

She stood up abruptly, gathered her things, and walked away. Salvatore stood watching her until she disappeared around the corner.

Chapter Sixteen

A Dead Animal

Caroline and Rosalia sat in the garden. The flowerbeds that Salvatore took great pride in attracted butterflies with their nectar.

"Some people say that butterflies bring messages from our loved ones who have departed," said Rosalia. "There have been times when a yellow butterfly has rested on my hand, and I like to think that is my late husband sending me a message."

"That is beautiful," said Caroline. "Let's test this out," she said, holding her hand out. "Hold your hand out too," she said to her aunt. They both did.

It was a beautiful warm day, and a cool breeze brushed against their skin. Caroline felt calm for the first time on the trip; her aunt had that effect on her.

Soon, a yellow butterfly flitted between them back and forth. The butterfly landed on Rosalia's arm.

"See? I told you," she said, smiling.

The butterfly then flitted towards Caroline but just as it was about to land on her hand, it circled and flew off.

"Oh dear," said Caroline. "That didn't look like it wanted anything to do with me. I hope Stuart is not mad at me," she said. "He died so suddenly. All alone. I sometimes wonder what went through his head. I never got to say *I love you*, before he died."

"I'm sure he knew how much you loved him," Rosalia said. "You were a good wife."

"Not a perfect wife," said Caroline.

"No one is perfect," Rosalia said. "Where is Julia?"

"She probably took a walk into town. She disappears now and again."

"I was hoping that Adela and she would get along. They are similar ages, but it doesn't seem like that will happen." Rosalia drummed her fingers on her lap. "Adela told me that she doesn't like her."

"That doesn't surprise me," said Caroline. "Julia is a difficult girl."

"Adela thinks that every attractive woman is after her husband. Julia is pretty so she is probably wary of her." Rosalia yawned. "I am so glad that at my old age I don't have any insecurities anymore."

"When did you feel insecure?" asked Caroline. "You are such a confident strong woman. I never would have thought that you would ever have doubted yourself."

Rosalia didn't want to talk ill of her dead husband. She had suffered his dalliances in silence because that was expected of a good wife where she came from. However, that pain was hard to forget. "I'm not such a strong woman, but I have learned over time that no one can make you happy but yourself."

"Auntie." Caroline flashed a nervous smile. "There is something that is troubling me. Please don't think I'm crazy."

Rosalia pulled her chair closer towards Caroline and leaned in, studying her face. "What is it darling? You know you can tell me anything."

"I have a terrible feeling… um… that Julia…" Caroline choked. "Is trying to kill me."

"Trying to kill you? Why would she do that?" Rosalia opened her eyes in shock.

"She wants me out of the way."

"That doesn't make sense. Julia would never want to kill you. Who kills anyone? This isn't a movie."

Caroline crossed her leg and nervously tapped her foot. "It's about money. I told you that Julia only will get paid out after I die."

"Yes, you told me that, but Julia and her husband are wealthy in their own right. Why would she be so desperate that she would think of killing you? It doesn't make sense."

"As I explained, Stuart left me all his financial assets to live on and use the money as I wish as long as I am alive, right? But she is obsessed that I will spend it all and by the time I die there won't much left. No one understands, but I know her well. She is a very greedy and jealous girl."

"Caroline." Rosalia winced. "I'm sure that Julia is not so conniving and evil. She would be *psicopatica*, psycho, if she murdered someone."

Caroline crossed her arms, and the tone of her voice was very serious. "She has attempted to kill me twice. I have proof." She was almost in tears.

"What proof do you have?"

"I took photos of the evidence. I know you think that I'm losing it."

"What, does that mean?" said Rosalia. "Losing what?"

"My mind."

"I don't think that you are crazy," Rosalia said. She cleared her throat. "You are just overwhelmed with everything. Stuart's sudden death has been a big shock for you. One's mind plays tricks under severe duress."

"Maybe I am nuts," said Caroline. "I also believe that James is here in Oristano, I heard Julia talking to him on the phone. I don't know what is real or not. Please don't repeat this to anyone."

Rosalia stood up and hugged Caroline. "Darling, why don't you go and lie down? A nap can work wonders on clearing your mind."

Caroline went to her room.

Moments later, as Rosalia was about to lie down for her afternoon siesta, she heard loud guttural screaming. Rosalia jumped up, her heart racing. It was Caroline screaming in horror. Rosalia raced down the passage and collided with Caroline running out of her room.

"What's the matter?" Rosalia asked, in complete panic.

"Look on my bed," gasped Caroline. "There is something foul on my bed," she screamed.

Rosalia ran into the room. On the bed was a dead animal. "It's a rat. A rat!" wailed Rosalia.

"No," Caroline shrieked. "It's not a rat. It's a cat!"

"Oh my god," cried Rosalia. "It's Chicco! Someone dug up Chicco! What crazy person would do that?"

"I told you," Caroline screamed. "Someone is trying to make me go crazy."

Salvatore heard the commotion from the garden. He raced inside and observed a scene from a horror movie. "Calm down" he said in a steady voice." He picked up the disintegrating corpse barehanded and carried it into the garden. He walked towards the ravine and hurled the body over the fence into the water below. Salvatore saw that the grave that he had made for the cat had been dug up with a shovel left lying to the side. *Who would do such a sick thing?* He washed his hands thoroughly in the sink outside before he came back in.

"Okay. I took care of the body. Let's all settle down."

Caroline clenched her jaw. "Obviously someone is sending me a horrible message." She burst into tears.

"Where is Julia?" Rosalia asked.

"She is not at home," said Salvatore. "I think she walked into town. Why?"

"No, nothing," Rosalia mumbled. She was too distressed to carry on a conversation.

"Should we call the police?" asked Caroline.

Rosalia shook her head. "The police won't do anything. They won't act on a threat. Like a dead cat on a bed," she said.

Caroline's whole body was trembling. "That's no help," she said. "What are they waiting for? A dead human body?"

Rosalia went into the kitchen, put the kettle on to boil, and made two cups of chamomile tea, one for her and one for Caroline. She knocked on Caroline's door.

Caroline sat slumped in an armchair staring into space.

"Are you alright?" Rosalia asked. "Here is some tea. That should settle your nerves."

"I think it was a mistake bringing Julia with me on this trip," Caroline said. "I thought that it would clear the air between us, but I was wrong. Things have escalated. Who else would have placed the dead cat on my bed? She really hates me."

"Sweetie, I don't think that's true," Rosalia said, unconvincingly. "Take a sip of tea."

"Maybe hate is a strong word," she said sarcastically. "She wants me dead, but not in a hateful way, a pleasant way to get rid of me."

They looked at each other and both cupped their mouths with their hands to stop them from laughing.

"I think I'm going crazy," said Caroline.

"Why don't you do something nice for yourself?" said Rosalia. "Take the day off tomorrow. There is a wonderful spa twenty minutes away in Bosa. The bus stop is close to our house it goes right into the town. You will love it." Rosalia stood up and stroked Caroline's hair off her tearstained face. "Our favorite restaurant is right across from the spa in the square. Pasta e Vino. I will give you directions. Go. Have fun."

Chapter Seventeen

James

It was about a year into the marriage and James wasn't happy. At first, he thought his unhappiness stemmed from his job. He worked in his father-in-law's law firm in Florida. In the beginning he was grateful that right after graduating law school he met Stuart who offered him a position in his prestigious firm. Stuart introduced him to his daughter, Julia, and James realized that the job came with strings attached. The message was loud and clear, date my daughter and if things go well, your work placement will be secure. James became aware that the job was a façade for an arranged match. Stuart had pinned him as a suitable husband for his daughter.

When he met Julia for dinner at a restaurant, arranged by Stuart, he was wowed by her. She was not only pretty, with a sexy figure, she was smart, cute, and had a sharp sense of humor. She laughed out loud at James's jokes. She listened with interest to his stories of his past. After a few dates that had led to satisfying sex. Everything pointed to a match made in heaven. However, it wasn't long before James started feeling a niggling doubt. He couldn't put a finger on it, but something wasn't right.

Julia was spoiled rotten by her father, she was never told the word, no. She also believed that she was always right. One would say, 'it's a beautiful sunny day', and she would reply, 'I wouldn't call it sunny, it's warm'. Or one might say, 'the food was delicious' and she would reply, 'I wouldn't go as far as delicious, it was tasty'. James could overlook her personality flaws because he was proud to have her on his arm, and she came loaded with money. But the one thing that James could not overlook was that she was mean. She was mean to waiters and mean to anyone that she deemed not on her financial or social level. She was a snob. James came from a comfortable, but not wealthy, background. He resented snobs and was intimidated by them.

James's parents did not take to her. His sister told him straight out, 'she is the biggest bitch I've ever met in my life'.

James was prepared to put all that on the backburner. He enjoyed nice things now that he could afford them. His parents lived in an unpretentious house in an upper middle-class suburb. They lived above their means to keep up with their neighbors. There were many times when James wanted the same things as his peers, but he knew his parents didn't have the money. When all his friends went to sleepaway camp for the summer, he stayed home. Most of his friends went to private schools but he went to the public school. When they all got their first fancy cars, he got his father's 15-year-old Volvo. His parents' blunder was to be the poorer folks in a wealthy area.

James became fixated on money. His excellent academic scores won him a full scholarship to Harvard. He vowed to himself that once he left home, he would never have to endure second-best again. When he met Stuart, he knew that this was his ticket to success. James was very charming and very well-liked by his peers. He dressed well, he spoke well, and he knew exactly how to behave in a country club.

Not long after they were married, James began to feel a longing for a child. He felt that a baby would be the best addition to his marriage. Becoming a father was something that he had always longed for. The idea of having a little version of himself, or Julia, lit a yearning in his heart. James found himself looking at babies, something he had never done before. When he saw a baby in a stroller he would look down and smile, and sometimes he would even talk to the baby in a cute baby voice and then feel embarrassed.

One day, James and Julia were in the mall, sitting at a café after shopping for clothes for their upcoming cruise. A young mother was spoon-feeding her baby in a highchair. "Yum, yum, yum," she said putting a spoonful of apple sauce in her baby's mouth. James was transfixed.

"James, I'm talking to you," said Julia. "You are staring at the baby. Stop it!"

"She's so cute," he said. "Look how she loves her food."

Julia rolled her eyes. "She's just a baby; they are all cute at that age."

James leaned in and said, "Wouldn't it be cool, if we had one."

"Don't start," said Julia. "I've told you a hundred times, that I don't want a baby now. We have so much we still would like to do. Travel, set up our home. We don't have the time for a baby right now."

"We could still travel. Other people do. We are fortunate that we can afford help, get a nanny. It all can be resolved."

Julia sighed heavily and blew her bangs out of her eyes in frustration. "Geez, James. It's easy for you to say. I'm the one who has to carry the baby for nine months. That's no fun." She looked down at her body. "Besides, I've worked so hard to get my perfect body, a baby will ruin that. My friends who have had babies all say that their bodies are never the same."

"I know you feel that way, but I have a solution," said James. "We can hire a surrogate. I have been doing a lot of research and it's not that difficult to organize. Let someone else carry our baby. That's a win-win situation. We get a baby, and you keep your sexy figure."

"That's very expensive," Julia said. "I've done research too. It's not that easy. You have to get a suitable match from an agency, she has to take hormones, implant our fertilized embryo which can take, or it can fail. There are all kinds of risks. We have to pay for all the surrogate's medical and living expenses."

"I know all that," James said. "It's very costly."

Julia drummed her fingers on her right thigh. "I could get three Hermes Birkin bags for that." She sighed.

"Here's a thought," said James, "we could ask Caroline if she would be willing to help pay for the expenses."

"I don't see that happening," said Julia. "I don't understand why my father left all his money to her. I really feel so angry at him."

"If she spends the way she is doing, there won't be much left for you after she dies," he said.

"I'm going to ask her to help with the surrogacy expenses." Julia lifted her head from her hands and bit her bottom lip. "Will she dare refuse us? Who knows? She may take pity and give us the money. The bitch always says how much she cares for me. Let her put her money where her mouth is."

Chapter Eighteen

Florida

Caroline felt nervous, she had to sit down and breathe to calm herself down. Julia had called the day before to ask if she and James could come over to talk to her. Since Stuart had died, she felt vulnerable and unsure of herself. After the conference with Stuart's attorney to go over his will, Julia had been very cold to her. In fact, she had not spoken to Caroline since. So, when she called to ask for a meeting, Caroline knew that it was not a good omen.

She had asked Mariah, the housekeeper, to set the table with a morning snack. Sliced lemon loaf, blueberry muffins, and a charcuterie board—all Julia's favorite things. Caroline had always gone out of her way to make Julia feel special. She felt sad that after all the years of building a solid relationship with Julia, it had all come to a halt over money. Caroline walked out onto the patio; the still ocean shimmering in the morning sun calmed her down.

The welcome desk called to say that guests had arrived and were on their way up in the elevator. When Caroline opened the door, Julia was overly effusive.

"Hey, good to see you," she said. She hugged Caroline tightly. *She wants something from me.*

"It feels so strange to be here without Stuart," James said, looking around the room.

"His favorite armchair is so empty without him," said Julia. She sniffed and wiped away an invisible tear. She circled around the room, her eyes darting. "The living room looks different," she said, "have you upgraded some things?" She studied the framed art works on the walls. "This is new," Julia said pointing to a large abstract painting."

"Would you like something to eat?" said Caroline. "Something to drink?"

"No thanks, we are watching our diets," said Julia.

"I'll have some of that cheese and salami," said James reaching over the charcuterie board. Julia rushed over and slapped his hand, "No, you don't need that," she reprimanded. "We made a deal that we were not going to eat in-between meals."

"Oops, you are right," he said, putting his plate back down. "I'll just have some coffee."

"Caroline, we want to talk to you about something very important to us," said Julia. She sat down on the sofa and ran her fingers lightly over the soft leather. "Oh, this is new," she said, "Roche Bobois? James, this is the furniture manufacturer that I was telling you about. That's what I want for our house. It's French."

"Well, how are the two of you doing?" said Caroline.

"Not so good." Julia sniffed, hung her head, and reached out to grab James's hand. "This is the situation. James and I, after much deliberation have decided that we want a baby."

"That's great," said Caroline. "You changed your minds? The last time you told me that children were not in your future. This is exciting."

"The thing is, I can't carry a baby. We have ruled that out. So, we are looking into surrogacy."

"That's awesome," said Caroline.

"There is a slight problem," said James putting his arm around his wife. "It's very expensive, and we just can't afford it right now." A muscle twitched under his right eye.

"I've heard that it is expensive," said Caroline.

"It's around one hundred thousand dollars," said Julia. "We would have to pay compensation to a suitable surrogate for her medical and living expenses. As well as for the inconvenience of the pregnancy."

"I get that," said Caroline. She looked them straight in the eye. "So, what is it you want from me?"

"To put it bluntly," Julia said, sucking in her breath, "we need your to help us cover the costs."

"Why would you need me to help? You can afford it."

"No, we can't," said Julia, her voice rising. "My father, for some unknown reason, was selfish and didn't leave me much." She burst out crying.

James stroked her hair. "Babe, take a sip of water," he said. He held the glass up to her lips. "Don't get so upset. We will work this out."

"My father stuck it to me," she sobbed. "You got all his money. It's not fair."

"I'm sorry you feel that way," said Caroline. Her voice quivered. She took a deep breath to regain her composure. "Your father did not stick it to you. He left you a million dollars. He paid off your house and left money to pay off your cars."

"What's a million dollars today? It's chump change." Julia's voice cracked. "We put it towards the house that we bought."

Caroline swallowed; she felt her face turn red. She was angry. "Your father wanted me to be secure. He wanted me to be able to live comfortably for the rest of my days. I only live on the dividends – the principal will still go to you."

"Only after you die," said Julia.

"That is true," said Caroline.

"That could take years."

"Well, that's not nice," said Caroline. "You should want me to live a good life."

"You should want *us* to live a good life," said James, clenching his teeth.

"I'm very hurt," said Caroline. "James makes a very good living from the firm. You both have a wonderful life. You can afford to pay for the surrogacy on your own."

"Are you saying that you won't give us the money?" said Julia. Her eyes narrowed and with lips pursed, she jumped up. "James, we are going," she said with a choked voice. "I have never met such a greedy person as my stepmother. A *real* mother would understand."

They marched out of the door. Caroline could hear the terrible things that they were whispering about her while they waited for the elevator. She sat trembling with her head in her hands. She knew that whatever she gave them would never be enough and it was very clear that Julia couldn't wait for her to die.

Chapter Nineteen

Bosa

It was as if a heavy weight lifted off her shoulders. Caroline looked out the window of the bus and all she saw was the turquoise ocean and green hills. She was pleased that she had taken Rosalia's advice to take a day off to clear her head. The bus turned off the road towards the town of Bosa with its pastel-colored houses perched along the side of the mountains like toy building blocks. Caroline closed her eyes as the bus driver wound his way up the narrow road when an oncoming truck almost pushed them off the ledge. Caroline cringed as she imagined the bus plummeting into the ocean below. A toothless man, holding a goat on his lap, roared with laughter. He called out to the driver, "Go faster, go faster, I love it when the tourists shit in their pants." The other passengers laughed with him. Caroline got the gist of what he had said in Sardinian dialect, and she didn't find it at all funny.

They stopped at the bus station in the square, Caroline's armpits were ringed with nervous sweat, and she had to sit down to regulate her breath. She saw the spa right away; it was in a white free-standing building with a French blue door. The sign read, 'Relaxing Spa'. That was an appropriate name for what she desperately needed.

In the darkened entrance, lit only with candles, an older woman greeted her at the reception desk. She was dressed in a white tunic with white palazzo pants, her dark hair pulled back in a bun.

"*Buongiorno, hai appuntamento?* Good morning, do you have an appointment?"

"No, I don't," said Caroline. "I would like a full body massage."

The women clicked on her computer and sighed. She clicked some more and sighed louder.

"Is there a problem?" said Caroline.

"We don't really do walk-ins," the woman said. "We are fully booked." She looked Caroline up and down. Caroline always dressed elegantly. She had on a floral yellow dress that was cinched in the waist. The flared skirt showed off her trim figure. She carried a woven leather bag and wore tan espadrilles sandals on her feet. Caroline must have passed the entrance exam because the spa lady picked up her phone and summoned a therapist.

A pretty dark-eyed girl came out the double doors and walked towards her. She introduced herself as Alicia and invited Caroline to sit in the lounge area to give her a brief medical history. The massage therapist filled out the information on a clipboard. She asked Caroline what medications she was on.

Caroline said, "I am only here for a body massage, I don't think I need medical clearance."

The older woman at the front desk called out, "Yes, you do. We have to know your medical history before we can apply any oils or creams on your body. That's our policy."

Caroline made up a list of drug names as they came into her head. "Relaxa 20 mg, Calmastatin 40 mg and Ragingmigraine 10mg."

"For such a young woman, you have a lot of ailments," the woman at the front desk called out.

The massage therapist led Caroline to a dimly lit cubicle. She told her to undress and get under the white sheets. Enya played in the background.

"Which are the areas you would like me to concentrate on today," said Alicia.

"My neck and shoulders."

Alicia rubbed lavender oil into the palm of her hands warming it before massaging it into her skin.

"Is the pressure okay?"

"Perfect."

"Where are you visiting from?" asked Alicia.

"From the States."

"Where in the States?"

"Miami, Florida."

"I have always wanted to go there. I have a cousin who lives in Boca Raton."

"That's nice."

"Her name is Luisa Maldonado. Do you know her?"

Caroline was silent for a minute and then shook her head. She was lying face down with her face in the donut hole. She wished that this woman would shut up.

"She was able to get out of this hellhole and escape to a better life. I wish it was me."

"Maybe one day you can go."

"I hate it here. I am so unhappy."

"I'm sorry," Caroline mumbled. "Alicia could you please be a little gentler?"

"I hate my life. Working here is torture."

"Um, I'm trying to relax," said Caroline through the hole.

"That woman at the desk, she's the boss. A bitch. I can't stand her."

"Excuse me Alicia, the pressure is too hard. Do you mind if we don't talk, and I can just listen to the music."

"That cow at the front desk keeps all our tips. If you put it on the card, we never get it, so can you please tip me in cash."

Caroline felt all her muscles tense. Alicia's voice sounded as if she was talking underwater. 'Sail Away' was on a replay loop and it started grating on Caroline's nerves. The room became too warm, and Caroline felt dizzy. She abruptly sat up, the sheet falling off her. "I'm sorry but I have had enough," she blurted out. "I have to go. I'm not feeling very well."

"I can feel that you are very tense. You are a very anxious woman. You should learn to relax, "Alicia said.

Caroline threw on her clothes, paid the bill, and darted out the door. Alicia rushed after her, "Don't forget my tip."

Caroline opened her purse and threw a bunch of notes at her.

Outside, she found a bench under a tree and sat down catching her breath. She had lavender oil all over her body, clothes, and hair. Caroline saw the restaurant Pasta e Vino, that Rosalia had recommended, she stood up and walked towards it.

As soon as she sat down at a table outside in the shade, a man walked towards her holding a menu.

"Good morning," he said jovially. "How can I put a smile on your face?"

Caroline realized that she must have looked glum. She straightened up, brushed her bangs, greasy with oil, from her face, and looked at him. He was possibly the most handsome man she had ever seen. The first thing she noticed were his white teeth against his tan skin as he smiled. Then his twinkling blue eyes. She also noticed that his collar-length black hair was sprinkled with gray. She presumed he wasn't as young as he looked. But still younger than her.

"I'm having a rough day," she said, "can you tell?" It would have been fine with her if he wrapped her in his arms and gave her a big hug.

"How can you be sad on such a beautiful day?" he said grinning. "You speak Italian very well for a tourist."

"And I thought I sounded like a local," she laughed.

"Coffee?" he asked.

"Coke Light with lots of ice, please."

"Anything to eat?"

"Something light. A salad? Tomatoes and mozzarella would be nice."

"Un insalata caprese. Perfetto," he said. "Where are you from?"

"Miami, Florida."

"I've been to Miami. I have a cousin there. Do you know the restaurant Dolce Vita? I helped him open that."

"I have heard of it. My late husband used to have his business lunches there."

"Why is he always late?"

"No, no," she cleared her throat, "*late* means he passed away—died."

"I'm sorry to hear that." He scanned her from head to toe quickly. "I'll be back with your drink in a moment."

Caroline felt herself blushing. It had been so long since she had been noticed by a man. He was just being friendly, but it was a treat not to feel invisible.

She was slightly disappointed when he came out with her drink and salad, talking on his phone. "Excuse me," he said turning away from his phone, "there are always problems with food delivery here." He placed her order on the table and continued to talk on his phone gesticulating wildly to make a point. He disappeared inside the door.

Caroline took out a mirror from her bag and reapplied her lipstick after she had finished eating. She wished that she had looked better.

"Sorry about that," he said, returning with a bottle of water. "This is my restaurant and every minute something comes up." He poured water into her glass and put out his hand. "Giorgio," he said, shaking her hand.

"Caroline." She noted that he was not only handsome, but he had a genuine warmth that put her at ease.

"The salad was delicious," she said.

"You have to come back for my pasta." He smiled. The corners of his eyes crinkled. "Where are you staying?"

"In Oristano, with my aunt. I was born there. My family immigrated to the States when I was a little girl."

"You can leave Sardinia, but Sardinia never leaves you," he said.

"You may know my aunt, Rosalia Rossi?"

"Rosalia and Salvatore! Of course I know them. They eat here all the time. I love them!" He slapped his knee. "That's why you seem so familiar, you remind me of your aunt. A wonderful woman and pretty just like you."

Caroline smiled; she was sorry when she was finished with her meal but there was no reason for her to stay on. "How much do I owe you?" she said.

"*Niente*, nothing," he said. "A niece of Rosalia's will never pay. Please come back so I can show you my true hospitality."

As Caroline walked away, she was aware of Giorgio's eyes following her. She was already planning to return for his pasta, *not to see Giorgio*, she told herself, but because she was really looking forward to tasting Sardinian specialties.

Chapter Twenty

Sardinia

Rosalia turned to Caroline while she chopped garlic for the sauce. "Did you enjoy the spa in Bosa yesterday?"

"It was wonderful. The massage was so relaxing," Caroline lied. "I feel like a new person." She needed an excuse to go back to Giorgio's restaurant.

"I'm so happy to hear that. You must go back again, as often as you can before you leave."

"That's a good idea," said Caroline.

"Sometimes we forget to take care of ourselves," said Rosalia. She placed the chopped garlic in the piping-hot oil on the stove. The smell of garlic filled the air.

"Mama, you should practice what you preach," laughed Adela. "You never do anything for yourself."

"That's not true. Cooking for the people I love makes me happy. I find joy in doing things for others."

"I need a good massage, maybe I will go with you," said Julia.

"I thought you found a spa that you like in town," said Salvatore. "The other day when I bumped into you."

"You met Julia in town?" asked Adela.

"I bumped into her after she went for a facial."

"I am the queen of self-love," Julia said. "I'm not ashamed to say that I am high maintenance. James likes me to look good. It's my full-time job."

"The smell of the sizzling garlic is making me hungry." He sniffed deeply. "*Spaghetti aglio e olio,* spaghetti with garlic and oil." He drummed his hands on his thighs waiting impatiently for lunch. "My wife is the best cook." Then he turned to Adela. "I want to ask you something, how is that friend of yours, the hairdresser, with the pink hair?"

"Pia?" Adela asked.

"Yes. She used to come around here often. I don't see her anymore."

"She is very busy with her hair salon… I don't see her much either," said Adela.

"She used to do a good job with my haircut, I was thinking of going back to her," said Salvatore.

"Who is Pia?" asked Julia.

"A friend of Adela's," said Luca. "No one special."

Salvatore ate his pasta and was very quiet. He rocked back and forth in his seat and looked pensive.

"What's the matter?" asked Rosalia. "Is the pasta not good?"

Salvatore shook his head as if he had come out of a trance. "It's excellent, dearest," he said. "As good as always."

"After we eat, we can all take a little siesta and then we will discuss dinner plans," said Rosalia.

"It's always about the food," said Julia. "You people live to eat. I eat to live."

"I think I will go back to Bosa for a massage," Caroline said.

"It must have been pretty good," said Julia. "It's not like Bosa is next door."

Caroline had been thinking of Giorgio since she met him. She was surprised by the impression he made on her. It was the first time that she felt any interest in a man since her husband died. She also cautioned herself that a younger, handsome, charismatic man like Giorgio would not be interested in her romantically. He was a friendly person and there was no harm in making a new friend. *It would be good a good diversion for me,* she told herself.

Chapter Twenty-One

Pasta e Vino

After looking disheveled and messy the previous time, Caroline wanted Giorgio to see her at her best. She washed and blow-dried her chin-length blond hair and brushed it to the side just skimming one eye. Although she was in her mid-fifties, Caroline had a girlish aura about her. Her alabaster skin was smooth apart from laughter lines around her blue eyes which sparkled when she smiled. A dimple in each cheek added to her charm. Caroline was tall and slim, and she aways dressed elegantly as if she was going to a polo match in Palm Beach.

This time, instead of the bus, she took a taxi to Bosa, and the winding roads did not unnerve her, they excited her. She arrived as the shops were re-opening after the afternoon siesta. She took her time browsing the shop windows. She went into a trendy boutique and tried on a number of outfits, to kill time. Caroline settled on a white cotton beach cover-up hemmed with white tassels. She bought a straw sunhat and a pair of leather sandals. Shopping bags in hand, she ambled across the piazza towards Giorgios's restaurant. Caroline didn't want to appear too eager to meet him.

The Pasta e Vino trattoria was empty, the regular diners would eat much later. A young woman with impossibly long dark hair tied up in a ponytail was sweeping the stone floor. She put the broom aside and greeted Caroline. "Table for one?" she asked. Caroline nodded. She was led inside to a table by the window. Caroline noticed that the woman had a beautiful smile. A few minutes later she came back with a basket of bread.

"Still or sparkling?" she asked in English, presuming that the Caroline didn't speak Italian.

"*Frizzante, per favore*, sparkling please."

Caroline looked around, there was no sign of Giorgio, maybe it was his day off. She should not have presumed he would be there.

The waitress came back to the table carrying a blackboard and propped it up in front of Caroline.

Just then Giorgio came bounding out of the kitchen, wiping his hands on his apron. "Signora is that you? What a surprise, you came back!"

"I came to pick up something that I ordered at a store yesterday, so I thought I'd stop in for your famous pasta." She smiled genuinely, happy to see him.

"I just made *Paccheri Norcina*, Rigatoni, sausage, porcini mushrooms and black truffles. I insist that you try it." He turned to the waitress, "Bring a bowl for the signora." He turned back to her and smiled broadly. "I have the best red wine from my neighbor's vineyard." He scurried out of the room, bringing back a carafe. He placed it on the table and poured her a glass. He poured one for himself.

"Do you mind if I sit down? It's early still, I am not busy." Before she could answer he sat down. He lifted his wine glass tapped it against hers and said, *Salute!* He took a swig.

Caroline took a sip.

"Isn't it excellent?" He beamed.

She nodded.

"I can't get over how much you resemble your aunt, Signora Rosalia. Not your coloring but you have the same smile," he said. "I knew her late husband Matteo well. Such a great man, I was so sorry that he died." He rubbed his hands together and clapped them, "well, that's life. Her new husband is a good man too. I'm glad that she's happy. So, you said that your—how do you say in English? Your husband is late now too? He must have been a young man. Was he sick?"

"He died of a sudden heart attack."

"Too bad," said Giorgio. "What did he do for a living?"

"He was an attorney."

The waitress came to the table carrying the bowl of pasta. She placed it in front of Caroline. "Parmesan cheese?" She asked before grating a heap over the plate. "Buon appetito," she said.

"Taste it, tell me what you think," said Giorgio. He peered at her wide eyed with expectation.

"Delicious," she said, and she meant it. The spaghetti was perfectly al *dente,* not hard and not soft, just right. The sauce was delicious. "Mm…" she said. "Yummy."

"I told you!" he said slapping his thigh. "You won't get better anywhere else."

"I love the truffles," Caroline said. "The flavor is perfect. I'm a big truffle fan."

"You like truffles?" he asked. He bit the bottom of his lip in thought. "I have an idea," he said. "How would you like to come with me truffle hunting? I need to get black truffles for the restaurant and it's the season. What do you think, Signora?"

"Where do you get them from?"

"Not too far. In the mountains. I know the area where they grow. It will be an interesting experience for you. It's not something that tourists usually do."

"Let me think about it," Caroline said. She was thrilled to be invited. "I will let you know tomorrow."

"Perfect," he said, that's a plan. "What would you like for dessert? We have the best tiramisu, it's famous across the entire island. And guess what?" He opened his eyes without blinking. "It's my recipe. I made it."

"I couldn't eat another bite. I'm sure it's delicious. I will try it another time. By the way, don't call me Signora. You can call me Caroline."

The restaurant was starting to fill up. As if on cue, Giorgio jumped up. He darted to the door to welcome the diners. "Good evening, my friends," he said effusively. "Come in, come in, we made your favorite dishes." They hugged and kissed him on both cheeks.

He is well liked and a friend to everyone, Caroline mused. An outing to search for truffles in a forest sounded like an excellent idea.

Chapter Twenty-Two

Truffle Hunting

Caroline heard Julia complaining about her as she prepared for her trip out.

Julia poured herself a cup of coffee from the pot on the stove. She was annoyed. "All of a sudden Caroline is Miss Independence, back home she can't go to the grocery store on her own," she said out loud.

"It's good for her, she is enjoying herself," Rosalia said. She punched the dough on the floured wooden table preparing to bake sourdough bread.

"Exploring old churches? Visiting farmer's markets. That's so boring." Julia bit into her cornetto, the jelly stained her lips.

"Why don't you go with her?" said Rosalia.

"That's not my idea of fun. I couldn't think of anything worse than traipsing around in this heat."

"That's why I didn't ask you to come with me," Caroline called out as she stepped out the front door. Caroline had a bounce in her step. She had not called Giorgio the following day to say that she would like to go truffle hunting. Caroline knew how to play the game. *Never let a man know that you are too keen.* Her hunch paid off because later that evening Giorgio called her to ask whether she had decided to go truffle hunting with him. Unbeknownst to him, she had already planned out her wardrobe. A white peasant blouse, blue jeans, and hiking boots. She arranged to meet him the next morning at the edge of town.

Giorgio pulled up in an open jeep, with his black and white dog peering over his shoulder. He was grinning.

"Hello!" he called out. "It's the perfect day for truffle hunting." He jumped out and opened the passenger door for Caroline. As she climbed in, he gave her a big hug. "I'm so glad you decided to come."

Giorgio drove with confidence gained from driving the route many times before. They ascended swiftly into the mountain ranges, hugging the edges of the winding road. Caroline did not feel nervous at all. In fact, she felt carefree and happy, something that she hadn't felt in a long time. The wind whipped her hair as she stood up, holding her arms stretched out wide like Rose on the hull of the ship in the movie *Titanic*.

"We are heading to Lanconi," he yelled, above the wind. "It's a little town bordering the forest."

Caroline sat back down, she nodded her head and pinched her fingers as the Italian sign for perfect. It was perfect. She never dreamed that she would be on a day trip with a handsome Italian. Caroline glanced at Giorgio; his perfect profile was etched against the stark blue sky like an ancient Roman coin. His strong hands clutching the steering wheel made her want to reach out and touch them, but she didn't.

At the top of a very high hill, Giorgio pulled up to a sandy clearing and stopped the jeep. The dog jumped out; he seemed familiar with the surroundings. Giorgio helped Caroline descend from the jeep.

On the left-hand side was the town of Lanconi, and on the right was the forest. The town looked straight out of a fairy tale. Wooden houses were perched along the hills as if they were about to tumble down. Despite the often-harsh climate, they had survived a century without too many problems.

Giorgio pointed to the path leading into the forest of oak trees. "We will hike for a little while, then stop and have something to eat and afterwards we will look for the truffles," he said to Caroline. He had brought a wicker basket and a red and white checkered tablecloth which he threw over his shoulders. As soon as they came to a clearing in the woods, Giorgio placed the tablecloth on the ground then opened the basket and took out sourdough sandwiches with mortadella and goat's cheese. He opened a bottle of red wine.

"This is so great!" Caroline enthused. "What is better than a picnic in the woods?"

"It will be even better if we find truffles," he said. "We use a lot of black truffles in season at the restaurant," he said. "Lucky for me that they are *abbondante,* how do you say? In this area."

"Abundant," said Caroline. "It must save you so much money."

"I don't worry about the money," he said smiling. "It's the good quality that we have here that makes me happy."

They ate in silence. The sun shone through the trees shooting dappled light onto the ground. Caroline felt that she was in an old flickering black and white movie. The dog's barking snapped her out of the reverie. Two men carrying shovels walked by. "Ciao Giorgio!" they called out, don't worry we will leave some truffles for you!"

Giorgio smiled. "We had better get going," he said. "My dog is a good hunter. He can smell the truffles – I have trained him well.

He pulled Caroline up by the arm and they made their way into the woods. Just a short walk up, Nero stopped, sniffed and wagged his tail. He ran back and forth from the ground to Giorgio. Giorgio used his bare hands to dig in the soft soil. In a shallow well, the truffles were snuggled together like baby bunnies. Giorgio pulled them out one at a time. "Beautiful!" he said. "Nice and big."

He placed them in the basket. A little further Nero repeated his truffle dance. "You dig them out," he said to Caroline. He handed her a small shovel. "This will be easier on your nails."

She used her hands. Caroline didn't want him to think that she was a spoiled princess. She pulled the truffles out one by one, feeling proud of herself.

By the time the basket was almost filled, they returned to the jeep.

"I bet you have never been on a date like this before," said Giorgio. He raised his eyebrows like a mischievous child.

"No never," said Caroline. She was pleased that he considered the outing as a date.

They climbed back into the jeep. Giorgio started the engine, and nothing. It clicked in defiance. He revved again. Again silence.

"It looks like the battery is flat," he said. He scratched the top of his head and looked perplexed. "This is crazy."

He rubbed his chin. "I guess we will have to walk to the village and get help. It's not too far, thank goodness."

Caroline nodded. She looked at her watch and could see that it was getting close to sunset. She hoped that they would get help to recharge the battery, and she would be back in Oristano before dark. It wasn't the time of day that worried her, it was having to explain where she had been to the family.

Giorgio and Caroline, followed by Nero running in circles, picked up their speed walking back into the village. The little stores that they passed were all shut down for the night. This was not a tourist town. The folk were early to bed early to rise, people.

They stopped at the only garage in town. "Damn," Giorgio said. It was closed. The lights were off. "Don't worry," he said to Caroline, "I will think of something." He did not sound very hopeful. "I'll ask at the hotel down the street if anyone has jump leads and can help us," he said.

The hotel was a small two-story brick building with a large neon sign in the window, *Aperto*, Open. They stepped inside; their eyes had to adjust to the fluorescent lighting. Sitting behind the reception counter was a tired looking man, with a cigarette dangling from his mouth. "Si?" he said without looking up.

"Good evening kind gentleman," said Giorgio. "The battery in my car is flat. Would you perhaps have jump leads?"

"Do I look like a mechanic?" he said.

"You look like a doctor but even a doctor may take pity on a stranger," said Giorgio.

"I can't leave this desk," the man grunted. He cleaned his ear with his pinkie nail, removed what he found, studied it and flicked it.

Caroline watched as the snot hit the back wall. She felt queasy.

"What are we going to do?" she asked Giorgio.

He put his arm around her and led her aside. "We probably will have to spend the night here and wait for the garage to open in the morning."

Caroline opened her eyes wide in shock. "I can't do that! What will I tell my family?"

"There doesn't seem to be another solution," he said. He called out to the man, "Do you have two rooms for the night?"

Caroline sidled up to Giorgio. "I can't stay in this dump," she whispered.

"Dump?" he said.

"Horrible place."

"It's the only one in town," he said. "A dump or nothing."

"I have one room left. The hotel is full – it's truffle season," said the man.

"Can the dog stay too?" Giorgio asked.

"There will be an upcharge for extra cleaning," he said. Giorgio nodded.

"Two beds?" Caroline asked. Her voice shook.

The man smiled for the first time. "One double bed," he said. He looked over at Giorgio. "You got lucky." He winked.

They followed him up to the room. Caroline was pleasantly surprised to see that it was clean. After the man left, she pulled back the covers to check out the bed. The sheets were clean, there were no stray hairs.

She called Rosalia. Her hands shook. "Auntie do not say a word. Let me explain. I went to Bosa this morning and Giorgio from the restaurant Pasta e Vino asked me to accompany him to look for truffles for the restaurant," she babbled. There was silence except for Rosalia's heavy breathing. "We are in Lanconi, his car battery is flat, so we have to spend the night here in a hotel until he gets it fixed in the morning." She stopped to take a breath. "Auntie? Hello?"

"Giorgio Lanconi from Bosa?" She sucked in a breath. "How do you know him?"

"It's a long story. I'll tell you when I see you."

"Is his wife there?"

Caroline gulped. "His wife?" She clicked off the phone. She looked up at Giorgio. "Have you told your wife that you are stuck here in the mountains?"

"I did," he said.

"With me?"

"Of course," he said. "Why wouldn't I? She trusts me."

Caroline surprised herself by the disappointment she felt. Why had it not crossed her mind that a man as handsome and charismatic as Giorgio wouldn't be in a relationship or married? She felt stupid and dumb, that was not the way she wanted to be. Caroline decided right then that if Giorgio was into playing games, there would be only one winner—her.

Chapter Twenty-Three

A Night in Lanconi

The first thing that Caroline did after she had inspected the sheets, was take the extra blanket from the closet, roll it up and place it as a barrier, down the center of the bed.

"Don't be afraid," said Giorgio, "I'm not going to touch you."

"If I had known you were married, I wouldn't have come with on this outing." Caroline sat on the bed with her arms folded and tapped her foot.

Giorgio shrugged. "Why not?" he said. "Just because I'm married, am I not allowed to have friends?"

Caroline didn't appreciate his smug expression.

"What century are you living in?" he said.

Without another word, she went into the bathroom, showered, toweled off and put her dirty clothes back on. She looked at herself in the mirror and decided that she looked like a wreck. Caroline felt foolish that she had thought there was a sliver of a chance for a hot and sexy liaison. *What was I thinking?* She pulled out her tongue at her reflection. *You are such an idiot.*

When she climbed gingerly into the bed, Giorgio was already asleep. *He has no worries*, she fumed. The good part was that Giorgio didn't snore; the bad part was that the dog, snored like a foghorn. Caroline covered her head with her pillow and finally fell asleep.

The crowing of a rooster woke her up. She had to acclimatize to where she was. She panicked when she didn't recognize the surroundings. Caroline looked around her to get her bearings. Giorgio was up watching the news on the TV, on mute.

"I didn't want to wake you," he said. He looked surprisingly refreshed, his hair wet and combed back. She noted how handsome he was.

"I'm going to get some coffee in the lobby, can I bring you some?" he asked.

Caroline was starving but she needed a caffeine fix promptly. "I'll come with you," she said.

There was a large silver urn with coffee on a side table and a selection of pastries on a platter. Two of the tables were occupied with guests. Giorgio carried their coffee to an empty table and Caroline followed with a plate of pastries. He took a sip of his coffee then a bite of his buttered croissant. "I needed this." He smiled.

Caroline smiled back. She decided that she had no reason to be annoyed. Giorgio had not misled her in any way, she was the one with the dirty mind.

"As soon as I've finished breakfast, I'll go to the garage and find someone to help me charge the battery," he said. "Did you manage to get some sleep?"

"I did," she said. "I was so exhausted."

"Good. That's what I like about you. You are so uncomplicated."

Caroline didn't contradict him although she knew that she was the opposite of uncomplicated.

"You are a good sport," he added. "Other women would be upset. Like my wife."

A suspicious look clouded her eyes. "Why would you say that?"

Giorgio looked thoughtfully. "You go with the flow. My wife is so dramatic."

She lifted an eyebrow. "You don't even know me."

A muscle twitched under his right eye. "I agree." He abruptly stood up. "Enough with the analyzing. I talk too much," he mumbled to himself. Giorgio nodded a greeting to the other diners. "Let's go get the car sorted out."

They walked up the hill towards the center of town and stopped at the corner at the garage. Cars were lined up for gas. There was a young attendant filling cars up with gas and another was cleaning windshields with a wet cloth. Sitting on an upturned bucket, drinking coffee from a tin mug was an unshaven man. He greeted them, squinting his eyes from the morning sun. Giorgio explained that he needed a jump start for his dead battery.

"Where is the car?" the man asked.

"Down the hill and around the bend," said Giorgio.

The man wiped his hands on his jeans, put his mug on the windowsill and told Giorgio to hop in his truck. There was only room for two. "Your wife can wait for us," he said to Giorgio, "with your dog."

One of the men in denim dungarees who had finished putting gas in a car turned towards Caroline, "*Buongiorno, signora,* good morning, can I get you something to drink?"

"No thank you, I just had breakfast."

"Giorgio's jeep is stuck?"

"The battery is flat, and we had to spend the night at the hotel. Do you know Giorgio?"

"Everyone knows everybody in this area," he said. "Giorgio is married to my cousin"

"Oh, I see," said Caroline. "We went truffle hunting for the day, and I didn't expect that this would happen to his vehicle. It's been very inconvenient for me," she said.

"Are you American? Your Italian is good for a tourist."

"Yes, I am but I was born in Orsitano."

"You wouldn't have known Giorgio or his wife, because you are much older." He scratched the back of his head. "Not that you look old, it's just…"

"I am much older." Caroline cleared her throat.

"My cousin, Bianca owns the restaurant with Giorgio in Bosa."

The young woman with the ponytail at the restaurant is Giorgio's wife. Caroline felt her face turn red. "Does she have long black hair?"

"Yes. A beautiful girl."

"I have been to the restaurant. She served me my food."

It wasn't long before the mechanic drove back in his truck with Giorgio following in his jeep. Giorgio jumped out, shook the man's hand and handed him a wad of cash. "Thank you so much," Giorgio said, pumping his hand. "I really appreciate it."

Caroline was just about to hop into the jeep when the garage attendant sidled up to her. "I will let my cousin know that I met you with Giorgio. I'm sure she will be interested." He strode away.

"What did he say to you?" Giorgio asked Caroline. She buckled into her seat.

"He said he will tell his cousin, your wife, that he saw us together."

Giorgio turned on the engine and soon they were speeding along the road.

"Hah! He is trying to stir trouble," he said. "Bianca knows that I went with you. She knows about the flat battery and everything. I called her immediately – I don't keep secrets from my wife." His voice was firm as if he was convincing himself.

"I find it interesting that I told you right away that my husband just died, and you never mentioned your wife?"

"You didn't ask," he said. "What difference does it make? Would you still have come truffle hunting with me if you knew I was married?"

Caroline shrugged. "I probably wouldn't of."

"I find that strange," he said. "I was only asking you to come with me on an outing that I thought you would enjoy. I wasn't asking for anything else. The fact that we had to spend the night together was not my doing, and of course nothing happened." He took his eyes off the road and looked at her. "Relax, I don't have ulterior motives, trust me."

Giorgio dropped Caroline back at her aunt Rosalia's house. When she walked in the front door, Julia said, "How was your little sojourn?" She smirked. "Did you and Giorgio have a good time?"

"A great time," said Caroline, "the sex was even better – hot and heavy."

"Eww Caroline," said Julia. She put her finger down her throat and feigned vomiting.

"I hope you are joking," said Rosalia. "You know better than getting involved with a married man."

"I was joking," said Caroline. "Don't you all think that I can take care of myself? The car broke down, what was I meant to do?"

"Did the car really break down?" said Julia. "That is the million-dollar question."

Caroline went to her room and slammed the door. She soaked in a bath to calm herself. When she got out of the bathtub, she felt depressed. It didn't take her long to figure out the reason for her dark mood. She was shocked at her inner revelation. *She was disappointed that nothing had transpired between her and Giorgio.* It dawned on her that if he had made a move she might have responded before she found out that he was married. Even so she decided that after all the trauma she'd been through, it was her time for some fun. *I deserve it,* she told herself.

Chapter Twenty-Four

The Proposition

In the morning Caroline's phone buzzed. It was a text. From Giorgio.

Giorgio: Good morning! I have something I want to walk by you. Are u available for a quick coffee this afternoon?
Caroline: Can you elaborate?
Giorgio: Elaborate?
Caroline: Tell me more.
Giorgio: It's a business idea
Caroline: Oh? Okay
Giorgio: How about Café Oristano, Piazza Garibaldi at 3 pm?
Caroline: Sounds good. See you then

Caroline was perplexed. *A business idea? That was so weird. This was a red flag. He is probably going to ask me for money.* She felt very disappointed.

Caroline didn't want the family to know her plans so she had to come up with a good excuse for going into town. "I'm going into town to pick up some Panadol at the pharmacy for my headache," Caroline said. "Anyone need anything?"

"Some tampons for me please," said Julia.

Now Caroline would have to make a stop at the pharmacy. She was becoming accustomed to the walk into town. At the beginning of her stay it had seemed far away but now it seemed much closer. Caroline had developed a daily routine and if it wasn't for the drama with Julia, she would have enjoyed her stay in Oristano. She loved being with her family, she loved the town and its people, and she loved the food. She could envisage living part of the year in Sardinia and part in Florida. She fantasized how much happier her life would be without her stepdaughter, watching her every move.

Caroline had to use her GPS to find the Piazza. The narrow streets were like a maze; if you didn't know where you were going it was easy to get lost. Caroline was out of breath when she got to Piazza Garibaldi. Right away she spotted Nero slurping a bowl of water at Giorgios's feet. He was seated under an umbrella outside the café. He gestured his location to her by crisscrossing his arms above his head. It wasn't as though she could miss him. Giorgio was wearing a bright yellow sweater, blue jeans and red boots. He jumped up to greet her. *He is either genuinely happy to see me or, he is a good actor.*

Nero was happy to see her too, he jumped up to greet her, licking her toes as she sat down. She ordered an Aperol Spritz; she needed the alcohol for courage. As soon as they were seated, she blurted out, "What do you want to talk to me about?"

Giorgio sat up straight, he brushed the crumbs off his jeans and had a serious expression. "I have a business idea, hear me out before you ask any questions."

"Okay."

He cleared his throat. "My best friend Claudio is thinking of launching a new anti-aging skincare line. He is experienced in this area and has had many successes in skincare. What do you think is the hottest anti-aging natural product to put into skincare?"

"I don't know. The buzzy ingredient of the moment is hyaluronic acid to retain moisture in your skin. But I'm not a skin specialist."

"Read my lips," he said. "Truffles," he mouthed.

"Truffles?"

"Yes, white truffles. As you saw, truffles are found in abundance in the area. At the roots of the oak trees. We dug up black ones, but in a different season, there are the white ones."

He sipped his Aperol, his eyes enlarged with pride as if he had invented truffles. "Now, hear me out. The *antiossidanti,* how do you say? Um… the antioxidants, vitamins and amino acids in white truffles help to reduce fine lines and wrinkles. It will take years off your face!"

"My face?"

"Everybody's faces. Caroline, believe me this works. I've seen it with my own eyes. My mother, God bless her, is wrinkled from the sun. She worked in the sun her whole life. She tried the first experimental jar of this. Poof! All those lines gone! She looks like a young girl!"

Caroline took a gulp of her Aperol. "Sounds interesting, Giorgio, but what has this got to do with me?"

"You are an elegant, classy lady, correct?" Giorgio stared her down. "A beautiful lady, an older lady."

"You were winning until the end," she said.

"Not older, you know what I mean. Not too young, not too old." He backtracked.

"And?"

"We think that you would be the perfect spokeswoman for the product."

Caroline burst out laughing.

"Don't laugh. Claudio and I want someone like you, who speaks English to promote our product in America."

"Giorgio, hold on a moment. I'm a busy woman. I am enjoying my life, why do you think I would agree to this?"

"We will pay you," he said. "We will pay you and you will get a percentage of the sales. All you will have to do, is film infomercials for us."

"Sorry, Giorgio, I have to say no. I don't really need this in my life. I am happy as I am."

"We will pay you well."

"I don't need the money."

"Give it to charity. Do what you want with the money. Please, say yes."

He was beginning to irritate her. Caroline stood firm. No meant no.

"At least just think about it," he said. "We can work on the project while you are still in Italy."

Caroline stood up. "I have to go. I have errands to run in town."

"Before you go," he said. "I have something for you." He took out a small plastic container from his backpack. "I made some truffle risotto for you," he said, handing it to her. "My specialty. Please taste it and let me know what you think. Don't share it because I want to get your opinion before adding it to our menu."

"Okay," Caroline said putting it in her basket.

"Can I walk with you while you shop?"

"Sure," she said, then immediately regretted it. "I have to stop in at the pharmacy."

"There is one not too far from here. I will show it to you," he said.

As they walked, Caroline noticed how well known he was in Oristano even though he didn't live there. People waved or called out greetings to him. Everybody seemed to like Giorgio, but Caroline was skeptical of him. He was married and he did seem to be pursuing her yet apart from complimenting her, he never made a pass. The one thing that she feared most about this meeting didn't happen. He did not ask her for money. In fact, he had offered her money. She decided to look at him with different eyes. At least to be kinder.

They arrived at the pharmacy and Caroline picked up pills for her *pretend* headache and a box of tampons for Julia. Giorgio insisted on paying for the items.

"It's totally unnecessary," she said, as they walked out the door. "These are my personal items."

He looked at her as if noticing her for the first time and suddenly reached down and kissed her lightly on the lips. Caroline recoiled and stepped back.

"I'm sorry," he said, "I didn't mean to frighten you. I just couldn't help myself."

"I have to go," she said, flustered. She walked away without looking back. Her heart was still racing long after she got home.

Chapter Twenty-Five

Acceptance

By the time Caroline arrived back home she had already made up her mind. She was going to take Giorgio up on the spokesperson offer. What did she have to lose? It would be an exciting distraction from all her angst and anxiety. This would be out of her comfort zone, which would be good for her. The old Caroline would have been suspicious and looked for red flags for reasons not to do it. The new Caroline threw caution to the wind and changed her question from *why* to *why not*? The thought of working with Giorgio gave her a thrill. She knew that nothing could come of a dalliance; he was too young, too cool and of course, *married*.

Caroline sauntered into the living room and the family immediately stopped talking and froze in their places. Caroline knew right away they had been discussing her.

"Where have you been?" said Rosalia. "We have been so worried about you."

She decided to tell them the truth. She was not a sixteen-year-old girl. "I was with Giorgio."

They glanced at each other.

"You know that he has a reputation in this town?" said Salvatore.

"A reputation?"

"Yes, as a playboy?" Salvatore scratched his right cheek. "He is one of the best."

"That's great," said Caroline. "I could do with a playboy in my boring life."

Salvatore's, Rosalia's, and Julia's mouths fell open.

"I'm a big girl," she continued. "I think I can take care of myself. Besides, I'm thinking of extending my stay for a week or two so I can take part in a business venture he proposed."

"I told you so!" Salvatore raised his voice. "I bet he has asked you for money."

"On the contrary," said Caroline, "he offered me money."

"Is that a joke?" said Julia.

"No. He has asked me to be his spokesperson for his skincare line."

Julia fell off her chair laughing. "You have to be kidding?"

Adela and Luca walked into the room. They visited their parents most days.

What's so funny?" asked Luca.

"My stepmother has lost her mind," said Julia. "She wants to do some business venture with a person she has just met."

"What do you mean?" said Adela. "Who?"

"You know that guy from Bosa who has the restaurant, Pasta e Vino?" said Salvatore, "Giorgio Lanconi."

"Giorgio?" said Luca, "Are you kidding? How did you meet *him*?"

"He is not a bad person," added Adela. "We like his food."

"He is not the kind of person you want to get involved with in business," said Salvatore.

"Calm down, everyone," said Caroline. Her voice cracked. "I'm not an idiot. He did not ask me for money. I am going to do an infomercial for his skincare line, that's it."

"Don't say we didn't warn you," said Salvatore more firmly.

"Goodnight, everyone," Caroline said exiting the room. "Give me some credit, I'm a responsible adult. I think I know what I am doing."

The following morning Caroline called the airlines to change her flight. She postponed her return to Florida by two weeks.

When she came into the kitchen, Julia was on Facetime with James.

"I changed my flight back to the States by two weeks," she told them. She turned to Julia. "You can go back as planned," she said. She poured an espresso.

"For sure, I'm going back as planned," Julia said. "I don't mean to sound rude, but I have had enough of this place."

James piped up on Facetime. "Babe, why don't you postpone too. There is no hurry for you to get back and you can work on your travel blog."

"Don't you want me to come home?" Julia asked, affronted. "You aren't missing me?"

"Of course I am, I can't wait to see you, but you are already there. What's another week or two?"

Caroline wanted Julia to leave as soon as possible. Not only was she behaving badly but she was causing tension for the entire family.

"I am going to be very busy with this project," said Caroline. "You are already bored. I'm sure you want to go back home."

"I have a big court case coming up," said James. "You won't be seeing much of me."

"I'll play it by ear, James," she said. "I'll see how things pan out here."

"Good idea," he answered.

Caroline had enough of Julia lying about James's whereabouts. She stormed up to her and grabbed her by the arm. "Why are you such a liar?" she blurted out. "Do you think that I don't know that James is in town?"

"Take your hands off of me." Julia's voice seethed with hatred. "What are you accusing me of now? You are totally nuts. Everybody knows that."

"You can stop playing games right now," Caroline said. "I know that James is not in Florida. You are both pathetic liars. I want to know what the two of you are up to."

"You need to see a psychiatrist," Julia said. "The fact that you can even think that James is in Oristano speaks loud and clear of your mental decline." She ran out the room, went up to her apartment and slammed the door shut.

Caroline was shaken by the confrontation. She knew that Julia would deny the truth. Julia was adept at deflecting accusations. Caroline would have to prove what she knew. In the meantime, she felt excited about the prospect of working with Giorgio. Even if nothing came of it, it was a thrilling distraction.

She did not feel fulfilled by her life in Florida. She always felt that she was playing a role and not living a life. She was the perfect wife and homemaker. She thought that she was the perfect stepmother and only recently found out how wrong she was. She went to her room to call Giorgio and tell him that she was willing to accept his offer. She hoped he would be delighted.

Chapter Twenty-Six

Drama at the Trattoria

A regular dining experience at Mama Sofia's Trattoria turned into high drama. Whenever Ornella and Beppe Accadi were in town, one of the few places they chose to eat at was Mama Sofia's. They were both very particular with their food. It had to be prepared exactly to their liking. They had to know where the ingredients came from and if the produce was locally grown. Beppe only drank certain local wines from his preferred vineyards. Mama Sofia was very honored that they deemed her restaurant good enough to eat in. Some eating establishments were rumored to be relieved that the Accadis did not frequent their places. Their difficult reputation caused more stress and havoc than their presence was worth.

At Mama Sofia's they had their preferred table, not in the front, not at the back, but towards the center of the room behind a column where they could view others, but others could not view them.

Salvatore, Rosalia, Caroline, Julia, Luca, and Adela had already made their menu choices for dinner, but Beppe and Ornella were having a tough time.

"I thought you said that you were looking forward to the *zuppa di pesce,* fish soup," Ornella said to Beppe.

"No, I changed my mind," he said.

"*The saltimbocca,* veal cutlet rolls?"

"Why would I want to eat that? You know I don't like to eat veal during the week?" His jaw clenched in frustration.

Mama Sofia rushed toward the table; she could tell that the waiter was getting nervous. If Signor Beppe wasn't happy then the whole restaurant wasn't happy.

"Signor," she said, "what can I tempt you with? I will make you anything that your heart desires."

"Calf's liver and onions," he said, "that is what I feel like."

"Um, we don't have that," Mama Sofia said. Sweat broke out on her forehead.

"In that case, I am not eating," he said. He puffed out his chest and folded his arms.

"It's not a problem," she said wiping her upper lip. "I will send Ernesto to the butcher."

"Dearest," Ornella said, "the butcher is already closed, please be reasonable and choose something else."

"When I say no, I mean no!" He banged his fist on the table.

Mama Sophia called out with a shaking voice. "Ernesto run over to Paulo, the butcher's house and ask him to open the shop for Signor Accadi. Calf's liver. Hurry!"

Ernesto wiped his hands on his apron and ran out the back door. At the same time Laura and her children walked in the front door.

Beppe turned white and Ornella turned red. The restaurant turned silent. The two children ran towards Beppe. They threw their arms around him.

"*Zio Beppe!* Uncle Beppe!" they cried, hugging him.

Laura walked towards the table. She was dressed all in white, with turquoise drop earrings and a turquoise pendant. She looked like an advertisement for a walk on a tropical beach. Her light brown hair tumbled over her bare shoulders. She wore no make-up except for bright coral lipstick.

"*Ciao amore*, hello my love," she said to Beppe in a syrupy voice. "Can me and the children join you?"

Beppe turned to stone. His eyes bulged and his mouth hung open. Ornella jumped up like a firecracker had been lit under her. She grabbed a steak knife from the table and, holding it like a dagger, ran towards Laura.

"Get out of here, you whore!" she screamed.

All the diners froze in horror.

Luca catapulted out his chair and restrained Ornella in his arms.

"I am going to kill you, you bitch," Ornella screamed, stabbing the knife in the air. "Leave my husband alone!"

The two children looked on in terror. Beppe put his arms around them, and they huddled into his chest.

"Someone is going to get hurt," said Julia. Julia sprung up, and raced towards Ornella, she pried the knife out of her hand. "Give me that, it's dangerous," she ordered with a booming voice.

Caroline raced up to Julia, "Give me that knife, I'll put it somewhere safe." She grabbed the knife, twisting it out of Julia's grip.

Then Caroline let out a bloodcurdling scream.

"What did you do?" she howled in pain. "Why Julia, why?" she cried out. "She stabbed me!"

Ornella and Laura froze, like in the game of freeze dance.

Someone called the police.

Caroline lay on the floor writhing and clutching her blood-soaked arm. "She tried to kill me."

"It was an accident," Julia whimpered. "I didn't mean it."

In the commotion, Laura grabbed her children and fled the scene.

The paramedics arrived. They bandaged Caroline's arm, placed her on a gurney, and pushed her into the ambulance that sped to the emergency room.

"It was an accident!" yelled Julia. "She made me do it!"

Drama in the House

The nurse in the emergency room stitched and bandaged Caroline's arm. Tears streamed down Caroline's cheeks, as she bit her lips in pain. Rosalia held her hand.

"Why is she trying to harm me?" she cried. "What have I ever done to her?"

A policeman sat on a stool by the bed and took a statement. He wrote down the details of what had occurred.

"This is the third time my stepdaughter has attempted to harm me," she said.

The officer turned to Rosalia, "I can't understand the signora's Italian, the grammar is incorrect, can you please explain to me what she said?"

"The stepdaughter stabbed the signora in the arm. Like she said there was an altercation in the restaurant that had nothing to do with the two of them. But Julia, the stepdaughter, grabbed the knife and plunged it into my niece's arm."

"And she said this has been the third time?"

"Yes. The third attempt at harming her. The first was a near-drowning, the second a poisoning, and now this." Rosalia closed her eyes and grimaced. "One more thing, there was a dead cat placed on her bed. It was Chicco, my cat, he died. My husband buried him under a tree in our garden. Guess what? Someone dug him up, the poor cat, and put him on my niece's, this lady here, on top of the covers on her bed. Can you believe such a thing?"

The police officer had stopped taking notes. With his pen poised in the air, he narrowed his eyes and squinted at Caroline. "Are there family conflicts going on?" he asked.

"Yes," answered Caroline. "I am in too much pain to go into it now, another time would be better," she said, grimacing.

He nodded his head, shook Caroline's good hand, and left the room.

Caroline called Giorgio as soon as she got home. "I have hurt my arm," she said. "I'm in quite a bit of pain. I don't think I can make the rehearsal for the commercial tomorrow."

"I am sorry to hear that," he said. "We can postpone filming for a while. Can we meet tomorrow to discuss our options?"

"Of course," she said.

"I will call you tomorrow morning to see how you are doing and if you are okay, we can meet for a coffee." Caroline heard him say to someone, "Our model is not well, please cancel the filming for tomorrow."

The atmosphere in the house was uncomfortable. Caroline and Julia avoided each other. Julia ate her meals in her upstairs apartment while Caroline sat in the kitchen.

Salvatore shook his head. "I can't believe what happened," he said. "I want to believe there is a misunderstanding and it was an accident."

Caroline excused herself to go and lie down and just as she was about to fall asleep, she heard a commotion from the living room. A high-pitched wailing made her sit up.

"Beppe wants a divorce!" howled Ornella. She had burst into the living room and collapsed on the sofa. Her head was thrown back as if she had been shot.

"What? What are you saying?" said Rosalia. She grabbed a box of tissues on the coffee table and handed it to her sister.

Ornella threw the box across the room. "He told me that he wants out of our marriage. Can you believe it? After all these years I have suffered, he wants out! That miserable, piece of shit."

"Why?" said Salvatore. "Why now?"

"I gave him an ultimatum. I told him that he has to choose between me or that whore. I will not play second fiddle to that homely, washed-out rag, with a body like a boy."

"An ultimatum," said Rosalia, twisting the corner of her apron. "That's not good."

"Whom did he choose?" asked Adela. "You or her?"

"Don't be stupid," Luca said to his wife, "can't you tell?"

"What am I going to do?" Ornella cried. "I gave him all the good years of my life. I was the perfect wife, even though he was a bastard. I never thought he would leave me for any other woman. Never." She searched for a tissue. Rosalia retrieved the box and handed her one. "He always said I'm the love of his life. He told me a hundred times, the others were just for sex, it meant nothing. Liar!" She spat on the floor.

Rosalia put her arms around Ornella as she rocked her back and forth in disbelief. "Tell me exactly what he said," she said.

"That he *loves* Laura, he is very sorry but that's the way it is. What does he know about love? He said that he found happiness for the first time in his life. What is happiness? I don't even know," she wailed. "Our marriage was just a lie. All these years was just a façade."

"Can you both not leave it as it is. It's always worked for you," said Salvatore.

"This time it is different. He has never been happy or in love before, not even with me. He is not capable of such things." She wept. "He wants a divorce."

"A divorce?" said Rosalia. The room became very quiet. "You mean, a real divorce?"

"Yes. Where you go to court and end the marriage in front of a judge, that kind of a divorce." The words came out flat and hoarse.

Rosalia studied the floor, she had never noticed how intricate the tile patterns were. She saw shapes she never had seen before, oblongs and circles in browns and beiges. The more she stared, the dizzier she felt.

Ornella's voice rose and fell. "He will have to pay dearly for this," she said. "Not only am I hurt, but I am also humiliated. He is making a fool out of me in front of the whole of Italy."

Ornella stood up and clenched her fists. She spoke a stern cold voice. "I will hit him where it hurts. I am going to keep Lily and Remy. I will fight for my life for them, that will kill him."

Chapter Twenty-Eight

A Business Proposition

Giorgio strode towards Caroline. She sat facing the entrance of the pastry shop. *He could be a model walking down the runway,* she thought.

He looked at her bandaged arm. "You poor thing," he said, massaging her shoulder. "Are you in pain?" he asked. "What happened?"

"I was in pain, but it's a little better now." She looked up at him and smiled. "Sit down and order something, I will tell you all about what I've been going through."

"A coffee and a *sfogliatella*, puff pastry," he called out to the waitress. Caroline had already ordered a coffee and a pastry. She couldn't use her injured right hand and was having difficulty cutting into her croissant.

Giorgio reached across the table, lifted her plate and cut the pastry into bite size pieces. "Did you fall?" he asked, leaning over and brushing the crumbs off her mouth with his fingers.

"This is going to sound crazy to you," she said. "As you know I am here visiting my family. I brought my stepdaughter with me. My husband, her father, as I told you passed away recently. I felt that we both needed a break."

"How old is she?"

"She is thirty-five, married." She flashed a nervous smile. "Her name is Julia. She does not like me. In fact, she hates me. She hates me so much that I believe she is trying to kill me."

A crease formed between his brows. "You can't be serious," he said,

"Unfortunately, I am very serious. It's a money thing," Caroline said. "It's complicated."

"Have you told anyone?"

"I told my family. I also told the police last night." Caroline showed him her bandaged arm. "Last night, she tried to stab me. Luckily, she only injured my arm."

"This is terrible," he said. He stroked the stubble on his chin. "Are you sure you aren't imagining it?"

"I wish I was," Caroline said. "Money does crazy things to people."

Giorgio leaned across the table; he brushed a stray hair out of Caroline's eyes. "I am so sorry you are going through this," he said. "I can tell that you are a good person, you don't deserve this."

Caroline teared up. "I know," she sniffed.

"If there is anything I can do to help, let me know," he said. "In the meantime, you won't be able to do the shoot for the product. As a spokesperson you will need to use your hands. You will have to hold the jar and apply the cream to your face." He picked up his phone and started texting. "I must just tell Claudio that you won't be able to shoot right now," he said.

"I know. I am so sorry," she said. "I was looking forward to doing this. I think it would be fun for me."

Giorgio was texting and paused. "You are the perfect face for our anti-aging product. You have great skin. You look young and healthy and carry yourself so well. You are charismatic, elegant and… sexy."

Her face flushed scarlet. "You are making me blush," Caroline said

"It's true. The minute I met you, I thought 'wow'. I told Bianca, I think we have found our model."

"Was your wife okay with that?"

"Absolutely, like I said before, Bianca and I have a trusting relationship. When we got married six years ago, we both agreed that we can do anything that makes us happy, as long as we are honest with each other."

"Like an open marriage?"

"Not wide open, a little open, just reserved for very special outsiders."

"That's very modern thinking," said Caroline. She didn't know what else to say, so she pulled out her compact and reapplied her lip gloss."

"Let me take you to see our manufacturing plant, it is very interesting."

Caroline nodded; she was eager to see what they were doing. They drove in his jeep along a sandy path. Giorgio's phone rang. "It's my wife," he said.

"Ciao amore," he said. "It's busy? Are you managing? How many tables are full? Oh good. I won't be long. I am doing some business then I'll come straight back." He made kiss sounds into the phone and disconnected.

They came to a stop in front of a small white warehouse. They jumped out of the jeep and entered the building. Caroline was surprised to see that it was a serious operation. Three men and a woman dressed in white coats, hairnets and gloves were bent over long tables stirring and measuring liquids. Giorgio called out to greet them. "This is my colleague from America," he said.

He led her through a double door that opened onto a large white room. The skylight threw ribbons of light over large bins filled with truffles. Caroline knew how costly truffles were and mentally did the math of the value of the inventory. Through a glass partition was an office, a young, balding man with round black rimmed glasses was on his computer at a desk.

"Ciao, Claudio, come and meet our spokesperson from America, Caroline."

Claudio stood up and shook Caroline's left hand. "Pleased to meet you," he said. He glanced at her bandaged arm but didn't say anything.

"I'm going to show the lady around," he said. "She can get an idea of our products."

Claudio nodded his head. Caroline could tell that he was a serious person, he did not smile or make small talk. If her first impressions were correct, she figured that he was the *brains* behind this venture.

Giorgio was proud of the project. He strutted through the warehouse pointing out the complex machinery and explaining the function of each one. When he showed her the showroom with the finished products lit up in glass cases, Caroline was impressed. Purple glass jars with gold lids were lined up in various sizes. They were labeled '*Crema di Tartuffi/* Cream of Truffles' in gold font. The merchandise looked elegant and regal.

Giorgio led Caroline to a white leather swivel chair facing a mirrored wall. He opened one of the jars and, taking her good hand, he gently rubbed the cream with his finger in circular motions onto her skin.

Caroline felt a thrill run through her body, a feeling she had long forgotten. He then lifted her uninjured hand and gently massaged the cream into the top of it. "Look how smooth your skin is now," he said. She nodded.

"Can I apply the face cream on you?" he asked.

She nodded again.

He dipped his fingers into the soft, emollient moisturizer and traced light upward strokes into her face. Caroline inhaled the earthy, sweet-smelling fungi potion and smiled. "I could get used to this," she said.

"We have put a lot of work and research into this product," he said. "I am totally committed to its success. I have seen the results with my own eyes, and it really works. So many beauty products don't deliver what they promise, but I believe that this one does. With the right marketing I intend to sell this to not only an Italian market, but international as well."

"That's wonderful," Caroline said. "When do you intend to launch this?"

He had pulled down the neckline of her dress exposing her skin and massaged the cream into her neck and shoulders. Caroline felt her body melting.

"As soon as we can. As soon as we can collect enough money, we will launch. We are ready to press *go*. I am working with my bank for a loan. As you can imagine this is a very costly project and getting the finances is the toughest part."

He pulled down her bra straps and massaged deeper into her shoulders, just where all her stress was locked. He lifted her head and cupped his hands under her chin.

"Caroline don't think that I am crazy, but the thought just came to me. Would you like to be my business partner?" He studied her large, clear eyes for a hint of interest. "If you invest some money, not a lot, we can build this enterprise together. I think we would make an excellent team."

Caroline recoiled and sat up straight. She pushed his hands away. She pulled up her bra straps and straightened her sleeves. "Is this what this is all about?" Her voice cracked.

She stood up and folded her arms. "Seriously, Giorgio, do you think that I'm stupid? You've been buttering me up, just to ask me for money. Wow. I wasn't born yesterday." She picked up her bag. "Take me home immediately," she ordered.

Giorgio was taken aback. He looked affronted. "I don't know what buttering up means, but I'm only trying to give you a lifetime opportunity," he said without enthusiasm. "I know why they say American woman have a bug up their ass."

"Interesting how all of a sudden you know all the English phrases," she said, seething. "How do you say in Italian— *you are a scam artist.*"

Giorgio looked down at his watch. "We have to rush because I need to get back to my wife and the restaurant."

They didn't say another word to each other on the drive home.

When he stopped at the house, Caroline got out and slammed the door.

"Asshole!" she yelled.

Chapter Twenty-Nine

Trust

Caroline walked into the house, threw her bag onto the sofa and sat down with her head in her hands.

"What's the matter?" asked Rosalia. She was a permanent fixture around the house, cooking or cleaning. Rosalia wiped her hands on her apron and sat down next to her niece. "Did something else happen with Julia?"

"No," said Caroline, "surprise, surprise not this time."

"Julia moved out of the house this morning. She said that she can't stay where she is being treated like a criminal."

"Good riddance."

"She took a taxi to a hotel in town," said Salvatore.

"How do you know?" asked Caroline.

"I followed the cab on my scooter," he said. "I knew exactly where she was going."

"What do you mean?"

"Julia has been visiting a small hotel off the piazza, I have been following her since you arrived. I have been very suspicious of her."

Rosalia stopped what she was doing and looked at him, shocked. "What are you saying? You have been following her?" She shook her head. "Why didn't you tell me?"

"I wanted find out what she is up to," Salvatore said. "Guess what?"

Caroline looked at him, puzzled. "What?"

"I discovered that James is in town staying at that hotel and Julia visits him on a regular basis."

Caroline was very quiet. Then said very slowly, "I knew it. I heard her telling James to be careful not to blow his cover. That is exactly why I am convinced that both she and him are plotting something sinister. "It's absurd to pretend he is in Florida. We've all seen him on Facetime." She shook her head in disbelief.

"He is not in Florida. He is right here in Oristano pretending that he is back home," said Salvatore.

"I asked Julia point blank if James was here and she vehemently denied it. She called me crazy and said that I need help."

"I didn't say anything because I was waiting to see what they are up to before telling anyone. I was trying to solve this mystery," said Salvatore.

"I don't know what's going on," Caroline said. "Are they both planning to kill me? This is getting weirder every day."

Rosalia exhaled, her cheeks blew up like a puffer fish. "Let us not jump to conclusions, there may be a logical explanation," she said, unconvincingly.

"I will get to the bottom of this," said Salvatore. "It's just a matter of time."

"I'm going to lie down," Caroline said. "I can't take this. I've had a rough day." Her arm was throbbing from the wound, "Aunt, can you please help me change the bandage?"

Rosalia followed Caroline into her bedroom. Caroline sat on the chair of the vanity table. Rosalia slowly unwrapped the bandage. Caroline's arm was still red and swollen. Rosalia rubbed antiseptic ointment into the wound.

"I think that I have to lay charges on Julia for what she has been doing to me," said Caroline.

Rosalia put on a clean bandage, then went to the bathroom and washed her hands. Caroline followed her then sat down on the closed toilet seat while her aunt redressed her wound.

"You can't just go to the police and accuse Julia of trying to harm you," she said. She washed her hands and dried them on the towel hanging on a hook. "You have to have evidence, before they will believe you," she said.

"I know," said Caroline. "We are also American tourists, so I don't know how that works. But then again, I am also an Italian citizen."

"It will be your word against hers. Why even go down that road?" asked Rosalia. "You may be wasting your time and energy.

A look of anger flashed in Caroline's eyes. "The girl is trying to kill me," she said with gritted teeth. "I'm not going to let her finish the job. I have to stop her in her tracks before it's too late."

"You are right," said Rosalia, "she has brought this on herself. Does she really think that she can get away with this? This will cheer you up, I am making your favorite seafood soup for tomorrow.

Rosalia's philosophy was, when in doubt, eat.

Caroline did not sleep. Thoughts whirled around her head. Her mind went over the ways that Julia had tried to get rid of her. She tried to think of different methods that Julia could plan. Would she push her in front of an oncoming car? Push her off a cliff while hiking? Julia had now gone to stay somewhere else and that meant there were fewer opportunities for her to do something.

Caroline was also unsettled that Giorgio had asked her for money. Her intuition had warned her that he might be using her, but her ego dismissed the red flags. Initially, when he didn't ask for anything, she had been pleasantly surprised. Did he really think that she was so gullible?

What Giorgio didn't know was that she had been thinking for some time about investing her money in something lucrative. Caroline had even consulted with her attorney back in the States about the legalities of investing some of the money that Stuart had left for her use. The attorney confirmed that if she invested just the dividends that were due to her, and did not touch the principal, then the profits would be hers to do as she wanted.

As she tossed and turned in bed, she had a revelation. Giorgio's offer was tempting. All she stood to lose was money that she could afford to lose and if it worked out, then she would have everything to gain—part owner of a skincare line. She felt her pulse beating in her neck. *The thrill of the deal was worth it*, she told herself. Her life had been so dull, and she was tired of always playing by the rule book. She decided that it was her time for an adventure! Time to make her life more exciting, that was if Julia didn't kill her first.

As soon as the sun rose and before she changed her mind, she texted Giorgio.

I want to invest in our venture.

There was silence then she saw the speech bubbles that indicated he was typing.

What changed your mind?

I think that u have a good product, and I would like to be a part of it. I want to be a partner in this.

There is no pressure. You have to be secure with your decision.

I gave it a lot of thought and I am sure of this.

That was a very quick amount of thought. Ha, ha. You made the right decision. You won't be sorry. We will talk tomorrow. Good morning partner!

Chapter Thirty

The Demise of a Marriage

Ornella was a mess. This was a woman who never left the house without being perfectly dressed and meticulously made-up. The minute she got out of bed, after her shower, she sat at her marble vanity table and diligently applied her skincare regimen followed by her make-up. Her face was her canvas, a little crumpled and withered, but after two facelifts and continuous injectable maintenance, she kept her skin looking much younger than her age. Ornella was very angry; in fact, she was furious. All her hard work of starvation and exercise to keep her figure svelte so that her husband wouldn't lose interest in her, was for nil. Soon after their marriage, after professing his undying love for her, Beppe strayed. That became the pattern. It took her a long time to realize that no amount of her trying to stay beautiful would keep him at home. He always came back but showed no remorse. He bought her an expensive piece of jewelry and expected her to keep her mouth shut. It was a mystery to all who knew her, and to herself the reason why she stayed with him.

"I like beautiful, young women, I can't help it," Beppe said, "but no one compares to you. You are the love of my life."

"Why?" she cried. "You break my heart over and over. Why?"

"Men are different to women," he said. He shrugged his shoulders and said as if in pain, "We need sex – it's our nature. I can't change the way we were designed."

Ornella had heard his theory a million times before; every philanderer tells the same story.

"Sex, with someone else," he added, "is like scratching an itch. That's all. The minute it's over, I never think of that person again. It's nothing, it's meaningless."

The problem arose when Beppe's die-hard philosophy took a sharp turn. When he met Laura. *That mousy, shapeless, bag of bones with crooked teeth.* Ornella seethed.

"The clothes she wears are from the department stores," Ornella told Rosalia. "She wears pants too tight and tops too small. No class at all."

"It makes no sense," said Rosalia, "Beppe is a distinguished gentleman with impeccable taste, why choose her?"

Salvatore joined the conversation; he was an expert on relationship matters. "When men get to a certain age, all their logic goes out the window. They are clutching at regaining their youth."

"Is that how *you* feel?" Rosalia asked. "Please don't come up with any surprises."

Adela chimed in. "Maybe that's why you bought a motorbike," she said to Salvatore.

"You may be right," he said, "but that's preferable than seeking a younger woman."

"I can get any sexy, young, hunk of a man," said Ornella. "Whatever I may be lacking in looks, I have in experience. And not to forget the biggest turn on of all, I have money." She ran her hands over her breasts and down her body. "My body is good enough, there are plenty hot young guys who like older woman."

Luca and Adela looked at each other, cupped their hands over their mouths to keep from laughing.

"What's so funny?" Ornella asked, annoyed.

Ornella looked like a crazy woman. Her blonde bleached hair had dark roots that fanned out like palm fronds. Her face was gray, and her eyes looked crazy. The only color on her face was smudged red lipstick that bled into the tiny lines around her mouth.

Rosalia handed her sister a cup of chamomile tea. Ornella's her hands shook so badly that the tea splashed over the rim onto the saucer.

Luca asked the wrong question at the wrong time. "What about the yacht? It has your name on it?"

Ornella caught her breath as if someone slapped her across the face. "The boat is mine," she said. "I will die before he gets the boat and changes the name."

"Don't think about that now," said Rosalia. "You will get everything that you want, because you deserve it."

Ornella hired the best divorce attorney from Milan. He had an office in Sardinia where he met his clients once a month. From the moment she met Massimo Garibaldi she disliked him. He reminded her of a Pitbull. He had a pugnacious manner with angry bulging eyes behind his orange, round-framed glasses. She reminded herself that she didn't need him as a friend; he was the perfect divorce lawyer —tough and mean.

"What can I do for you?" he asked. He scanned her from head to toe, then gestured for her to sit down across from the large wooden desk.

"My husband has left me for his mistress," Ornella said, her eyes welling up with tears.

"What do you want to do about it?" he asked while taking notes on a pad.

"I need to divorce him," she said, "that's why I am here."

"And your husband? He wants to stay married because it's cheaper?"

"No. He was the one who brought up the divorce."

"I looked up your husband's financial situation after you called to make this appointment. He is in good shape," he said. He buzzed his secretary over the intercom. "Two espressos, please," he said. "You are in a good position. Your husband has a replacement for you already waiting in the wings. That's a good thing.

The assistant carried in the coffee and placed one in front of the attorney and one in front of Ornella. "Grazie," Attorney Garibaldi said, and dismissed her with a wave.

"Is there anything you can think of that will punch him in the guts that we can use for leverage?" he asked.

"Mm…. Yes, the dogs. Lily and Remy. We don't have children. They are our children. I want custody of my babies. He will fight me for them."

"That's it?" he said.

She nodded.

"Well okay then. My assistant will give you a breakdown of my fees and retainer. Then we will go ahead and file for the divorce. Thank you, Signora." He put out his hand, shook her hand tightly, and led her out the office into the lobby.

Before she left his office, Ornella glanced at the pad where he had been taking notes, not one word was written—only doodles of slanted eyes and broken hearts.

"I have heard of Beppe Accadi," he said as he pressed the elevator button for her. "Who hasn't? All I can tell you is good riddance to bad rubbish."

Chapter Thirty-One

The Hair Salon

Caroline walked into town to get her hair trimmed and highlighted. Rosalia had recommended her hairdresser and made the appointment for Caroline. Now that Caroline had extended her stay in Sardinia, she was overdue for her color maintenance. Caroline had the last appointment of the day, which was the only opening available. The salon wasn't busy, and the front desk receptionist was watching a reel on her phone. She greeted Caroline without taking her eyes off the screen. "Pia, your client is here," she called out to the stylist sitting on her chair filing her nails.

The pink-haired young woman, covered in tattoos, jumped up and introduced herself to Caroline. After Caroline was seated on the chair facing a mirror, they discussed what her hair styling options would be.

The stylist ran her hands over Caroline's hair, lifting pieces and fluffing them up.

"Your hair needs a trim and also a conditioning treatment. We will do that after the highlights." She shook her head slowly and looked irritated. "Where do you regularly get your hair done?" She asked.

"In Florida, Miami, where I live," Caroline answered. "I go to a top hair stylist. In fact, he is Italian."

She pursed her lips and sighed. "Your hair is in pretty bad shape," she said. "Over-bleached, split ends, and a bad cut."

"I didn't think it was that bad," said Caroline. "I actually like my cut and color."

"Not to worry," she said. "I will try my best to fix this mess. That's what I do. I'm known as the hair magician in this area."

She placed a black plastic cape over Caroline's shoulders. Then she disappeared into a room at the back and reappeared with a small black bowl filled with purple paste. Pia had a pile of foil squares on the cart next to her. She sectioned Caroline's hair and applied the paste on each strand with a brush, then wrapped them in foil.

"What brings you to Oristano?" Pia asked.

"My aunt and her family live here," she said.

"Who is you aunt?"

"Signora Rosalia."

"Adela's mother?"

"Yes. She made my hair appointment for me. Do you know them?"

"Of course," she said. "Everyone knows everyone in this town. Adela and Luca are friends of mine."

"IcamewithmydaughterJulia,well,mylatehusband'sdaughter."

"That's nice." She brushed the bleach on the remaining strands so firmly that the foil tore. "Ugh," she mumbled as she redid them.

Caroline's head was covered in silver foil packages that stood out, giving her the appearance of a space alien.

Pia threw some magazines onto Caroline's lap, set a timer and told her to chill out for a while.

Pia disappeared behind a screen. There was one other client having her hair blow-dried. She and her stylist were having a lively conversation about the trials and tribulations of dating.

Caroline heard her name being mentioned from behind the screen. She cocked her head to listen. Pia was talking to someone in Italian. It was a one-way conversation, so Caroline knew she was on the phone. She didn't even think that Pia knew her name and why was she talking about her?

"I am shaking," Pia said. "Can you believe it? She came in for her hair. I'm dying!"

There was a break in the conversation then Pia continued, "Adela, my god what are the chances? Yes, yes, I will still meet you and Luca this evening. Of course. See you later."

Caroline thought, *why is she talking to Adela and Luca about her? Why would she be of interest to them?"*

Pia came to check on Caroline's color. She removed the foil pieces.

"It's ready" she said. "Come to the sink."

Caroline reclined on the chair and leaned her head back against the edge of the sink. Pia removed the rest of the foils from her head. She then rinsed off the paste with hot water and sprayed Caroline's head including her neck and shoulders. Water dripped down inside her cape.

"Is the temperature okay?" Pia asked.

"It's a bit hot. Actually, it's very hot." Caroline inhaled and held her breath.

"Oops," Pia said and turned on the cold water, spraying Caroline's face. She then mopped up the droplets with the corner of a towel, smudging Caroline's make-up. She massaged shampoo into her head using both hands as if she was washing a stained piece of laundry. Pia rinsed the hair, twisting Caroline's neck firmly, from side to side.

"Have you had a rough day?" asked Caroline.

"Why do you ask?"

"You seem a bit tense," said Caroline.

Pia wrapped Caroline's hair tightly with a towel into a turban and led her back to the chair. Pia trimmed the ends of her hair, rubbed in a mousse to add body to the hair, and blow-dried each strand using a big round brush. Caroline was pleased with the results. The color was perfect, the highlights blended with her natural darker shade of blonde and the cut of her shoulder length bob was perfection. Although Caroline was upset by Pia's aggressive manner and rude attitude, she had to admit that the end product was exceptional. She complimented Pia, paid at the desk and left a sizable tip. Pia didn't say thank you or goodbye.

Caroline went across the street to a little coffee bar and stood at a high-top table. She needed the caffeine for an energy boost. She was feeling lethargic. As she looked up, she saw Pia leaving the salon, talking on her phone. Caroline felt unsettled about the connection of Pia to Adela. She gulped down the rest of her espresso, put her empty cup on the table and decided to see where Pia was going. She followed her. The stores were shutting down for the night, but many people were around. That made it easier for Caroline to remain undetected. Pia walked into a small trattoria on a corner of a quiet alley. Caroline stood behind a tree and soon enough Julia arrived at the trattoria with three others. Caroline gasped, she was with James, Adela and Luca.

Why would Pia, Julia, James and Luca be meeting together at a restaurant? Nothing made sense.

Chapter Thirty-Two

Bosa

It was another hot day when Caroline took a taxi to Bosa. She had to ask the driver to turn on the air conditioner. Her perfectly styled hair was damp, and her bangs stuck to her forehead. The driver said he couldn't afford to run the air and told her to open the window. The hot air blowing in made it worse. Earlier, on her way out to the taxi stand, Rosalia and Salvatore asked where she was going. She told them the truth.

"I'm meeting up with Giorgio in Bosa to discuss a business proposition," she said.

They looked at each other as if she had told them that a beloved was dying.

"I beg of you," said Rosalia. She put her hands together as if she was praying. "Don't get involved with him. You will lose all your money."

"What is the business about?" asked Salvatore.

"A skincare line. Anti-aging creams and serums using truffles as the main ingredient."

"What does Giorgio know about beauty products?" asked Rosalia, "he is a cook, he knows food. He is in the restaurant business." Rosalia, kneading dough on the kitchen table, stopped and punched it hard.

"His wife runs the business side," said Salvatore. "Be careful Caroline, don't let people swindle you out of your money."

"I'm totally capable of taking care of myself," said Caroline, affronted. "I know what I am doing."

Rosalia and Salvatore both shook their heads. "Don't say we didn't warn you," they said.

Caroline had already weighed up the pros and the cons. She had factored in the possibility of losing her investment money, but it was the excitement of the venture that to her was worth every penny. Caroline's eyes were wide open to the situation, including that Giorgio was married, but the thrill of the chase was alluring to her. She hadn't felt this alive in years, and besides, she did believe in the product. It made sense and it could work. The beauty industry was a billion-dollar market, and she wanted a piece of it.

Caroline and Giorgio were to meet in the historic center at a small seafood trattoria, just below the imposing Malaspina Castle. He seemed to favor wearing bright colors and as usual he did not disappoint. She could see him from the other side of the piazza —he wore a white shirt, green jeans, and bright turquoise loafers. Giorgio waved to her as she approached, he stood up to hug and kiss her on both cheeks.

"How beautiful you are!" he exclaimed.

She wanted to reply, 'how handsome you are!' but she held back because she didn't want him to know how taken she was with him. Caroline was relieved to see that their table was in the shade under a large awning and beside a huge electric fan. As soon as she sat down, Giorgio poured her a glass of white wine and turned his full attention to her.

"I can't tell you how excited I have been since you agreed to invest in this venture." He leaned over and took her hand. "Caroline, this is going to be huge, I feel it in my ribs. And you are the perfect partner for me."

"Why do you think that?" she said. She sipped her wine leaving a red lipstick stain on the rim of her glass.

"From the minute I met you, I was speaking to myself—this magnificent woman is beautiful, smart and… how you say?"

"Has money?" Caroline suggested.

"Yes, that too, but you have a special quality. Money I can find anywhere but someone like you, impossible."

"Do you have a business plan I can look at?"

"Of course. I will email it to you so you can go over it."

"Before I agree to anything, I have to talk to an attorney," Caroline said.

"Yes, yes, naturally, of course, you will know everything. I am an open briefcase."

"Open book," Caroline said.

"Yes, book. Forgive my English, it's not so good." He looked at the menu on the blackboard placed in front of their table. "You must be hungry, let's eat," he said.

"I just want the seafood salad," Caroline said. She wasn't hungry but she had felt that she had to order something.

Giorgio ordered a dozen oysters. "Are you sure you don't want oysters?" he asked, "Maybe just a few?" he added. "You know what oysters do?" He winked.

"Yes, I'm aware of their reputation, that's why I'm not ordering them today." She smiled.

He pulled an exaggerated sad face. "That's telling me off," he said. "I'm sure that I wouldn't need oysters if I was with you."

Caroline choked on a piece of bread and coughed.

"You are so shy." He laughed. "That's so cute."

They watched some young boys kicking a soccer ball around the piazza. "Children are so simple," Caroline said, changing the subject. "Look how they play, as if they don't have a care in the world."

"This is before life gets in the way and messes them up," Giorgio said.

"Has life had that effect on you?" she asked. Caroline broke a piece of her bread and dipped it in the olive oil then took a bite.

"I have had my bad times," he said. He held the edge of an oyster shell and slurped the oyster down. "But I have had many good times too. And you?"

"I am going through a bad time right now, "Caroline said. "My life is in danger, as we speak."

"You told me. You believe that your stepdaughter wants to harm you."

"I don't believe," she said. "I know."

"If I can do anything to help you, just let me know." He drummed his fingers on his thighs and looked serious when he said, "Caroline, you are becoming special to me. I won't let anything bad happen to you."

She looked him straight in the eyes and said, "Giorgio please don't talk crap. You are a married man and if we are going to do business together then that's what we have to be, business partners."

"I know how you feel," Giorgio said, "that's why I like you. You are a woman of morals. I agree with you, but my wife and I are married in name only. She needed a visa to stay in Italy, she is from Montenegro, and we married so she can stay here."

"Enough of that," Caroline said. "Let's get down to business. How much money are we talking about?"

"I have done the beginning numbers, and it's not that much. I already have some of the basic machines, we need more, the ingredients and the staff to begin the manufacturing. If we each put in US $100,000 that should be enough to start with."

"It all has to be legal and signed," said Caroline with pursed lips.

"*Ovviamente*, of course," he said. He reached over for Caroline's hand. "Let's shake it up," he said. "To a wonderful partnership." He pumped her hand.

Before you go back to Oristano, I want to show you the beautiful Temo river." He pulled her up by her hand. "We can go for a little walk along the banks."

"I do have to get back," said Caroline. "We can leave it for another day."

When the check came, Giorgio patted his shirt pockets, then his pants, "I seem to have left my wallet at home," he said. "Can you settle this, and I will pay you back?"

"Yes," said Caroline, "no problem." She saw red flags waving in her face, and instead of paying attention, she paid the bill, kissed Giorgio lightly on the lips, and hurried away.

Chapter Thirty-Three

It's Gone to the Dogs

"They stole my ring," Caroline said to her mother. Her mother did not look up. She patted her toy puppy on its head in slow rhythmic motions. "Do you remember my diamond ring that Stuart gave me on our tenth anniversary?" Her mother burped. "The ring you said that was bigger than Elizabeth Taylor's. Well, it's missing."

Her mother stroked the toy puppy's back. She was staring into space as if she was watching an old home movie from her past but couldn't figure out who was who.

"Well guess what, Mama?" Caroline turned her mother's head to face her. "My real ring is in my security box at the bank. The joke is on them. I was wearing a replica ring. Who in their right mind would bring a real diamond on vacation?" Caroline smirked. "So, whoever stole my ring, and I know it's Julia, is in for a big shock."

A caregiver tapped on the door, "Signora, here is your lunch," she said to the old lady. She greeted Caroline, "I am going to feed the signora." She pulled the hospital table across her mother's lap and placed the tray on it.

"I'll feed my mother," said Caroline.

"Are you sure?"

"Of course. It's my pleasure."

"You have to have a lot of patience," the caregiver said, "the signora is very stubborn. Sometimes she won't open her mouth."

"I'll try my best," Caroline said. "Thank you so much for all that you do. I appreciate how well you take care of her."

"*Lei e una stronza*, she is a bitch," said her mother in a surprisingly clear, strong voice. "She stole my ring."

"I'm sorry," Caroline said turning red. She knew that her mother didn't have any jewelry at the assisted living facility.

"That's okay," said the caregiver. "I'm used to it. It's her way of showing affection."

There was a light tap on the door and the head nurse carrying a clipboard stepped in the room.

"*Bongiorno Signora*, good day," she said to Caroline. "It's so nice to see you here again. Your mother is doing great, everyone here just loves her."

The old lady looked up. "She stole my ring," she said. She pointed at the caregiver.

"I'm so sorry," said Caroline, "I know it's not true. We were talking about rings, so I think that triggered her."

The head nurse wrote on her clipboard. "We realize that our patients can make false claims, but we take what they say seriously until proven otherwise," she said. "Don't worry we are used to this." She left the room.

Caroline cut up the chicken into small pieces and fed it to her mother from a spoon. Her mother opened her mouth like a baby bird. Caroline felt pangs of sadness, about how their roles had turned. Her mother was now like an infant.

"Mama, people are trying to get rid of me," she said. "All for greed. You can't trust anyone. Even the ones I thought loved me." She placed a spoon of rice in her mother's mouth. "But don't worry about me, Mama. I can look after myself. You always taught me that."

When Caroline arrived back home, the family were seated around the kitchen table. Caroline marveled how they looked like a typical happy family chatting after a meal. No one would imagine the underlying tensions and conspiracies. Adela greeted her as if she was her favorite cousin. Luca poured a glass of red wine and handed it to her. *These were two people plotting something ominous behind my back,* she mused. *Julia, James and the hairstylist, Pia meeting up with them in secret. Why?* Caroline was not going to confront them. She knew that they would come up with some fake excuses.

Everyone's attention was on Ornella. She was the main character of the soap opera. She pounded a fist on her large bosoms and cried out, "My life is over. Please, please someone shoot me. I beg of you. Do me a favor. I'd rather be dead than going through what I'm going through now."

Rosalia wrapped her arms around her sister. "No, no. Don't talk like that. Your life is not over. Everything will turn out for the better."

"I am finished," cried Ornella.

"My darling, God works in mysterious ways," said Rosalia, "we don't know His plans."

"I am being punished. I must have done something wrong in my past. My husband is torturing me. Beppe is hitting me with the one thing that I care most about, my babies. Not only has he left me for *un pezzo di merda*, a piece of shit, he now wants to take away the puppies."

"What does your attorney, Garibaldi, say?" asked Rosalia.

"He advises that we have to split custody of Remy and Lily. One week with me, one with the bastard."

"That sounds fair," said Salvatore.

"It's terrible for the doggies." Ornella blew her nose loudly. "This back and forth will destroy them emotionally. I hired a dog psychologist who has written a book about this. He is prepared to be a witness in court."

"We should all have such problems," said Caroline under her breath.

Everyone at the table turned around and gaped at Caroline in horror.

"What did you say?" said Ornella.

"I said, you have a big problem. I have a big problem too. Someone is trying to kill me."

"Caroline, sorry I have to tell you this, you are being paranoid," Adela said. "Why would anyone want to kill you?"

"I am not paranoid. I have the proof."

"Speaking of psychologists," said Luca. "With all due respect, I think you should see one."

"If anything happens to me, look into my stepdaughter and her husband, James," Caroline said.

"Stop!" said Rosalia. "We are all too emotional and are saying things that we don't mean." She checked her watch. "It's time for a siesta and when you wake up things will look better." She turned to Ornella. "You and I will go to mass and pray for the dogs. Beppe isn't capable of taking good care of them."

Chapter Thirty-Four

The Factory

The skincare facility was impressive. Everything was painted white. The walls, the floors, even the ceilings. The work counters were white as well as the stools. It looked like a castle made of ice. All the lab technicians wore white from head-to-toe. Only their goggles were black.

"It looks very clean and hygienic," the banker said to Giorgio and Caroline.

"It has to be," Giorgio said. He was showing the newly built factory to two men from the loan department at a local bank. Both were young and dressed casually in white shirts and blue jeans.

"We are dealing with high-end skincare, and we are conducting clinical trials."

"Not on animals I hope," said the taller man.

"Absolutely not, this is a vegan, cruelty free product."

Giorgio was hoping to get an additional small business bank loan for the project. He had explained to Caroline that the extra funding would take some of the financial pressure off them.

They toured the huge metallic vats in the climate-controlled hall where the emollient cream was stored. It could have been a milk factory churning fresh cream. The main difference was the smell of freshly dug truffles.

After the tour, the men shook hands with Giorgio and Caroline. "We will get back to you shortly," they said.

"I could tell that they were impressed," said Giorgio, "I'm confident that we will get the loan that we are asking for."

"If we do, would the amount we are putting in be reduced?" Caroline asked.

"It's a costly enterprise," Giorgio said. "The more capital we have the better position will be in."

They walked towards his jeep. "I have a treat for us," he said. "If it suits you, I packed a picnic lunch for us."

Caroline looked at the time on her phone. She checked her calendar although she knew that she had no plans. "I am free," she said. "That would be nice."

"We will go to the Temo River. There are nice places along the banks to have a picnic," he said.

He put his arm around her as they walked to the jeep. Caroline had already been on a picnic with Giorgio so she knew that the food choices would be delicious. Even the blanket was special, a soft cashmere. When they arrived at the grassy stretch, Giorgio unpacked the wicker basket. He spread out an array of artisanal breads, a selection of cheeses, and sliced meats. He also had a bowl of fresh figs stuffed with goat cheese. Caroline was impressed by his self-confidence of having planned an elaborate picnic spread before he knew that she would agree to join him.

"This is amazing," she said. "What if I would have said I couldn't go?"

"I would have taken the food home," he said.

"Your wife would have been happy."

"But I would have been sad." He moved closer to her.

"Giorgio, I am really uncomfortable that you are married."

He ran his fingers lightly down her arms. "I told you that I was married from day one. I have nothing to hide. I also explained to you that my relationship with my wife is like, how do you say? *Convenienza?*

"Convenience," she said.

"Yes. If you are not comfortable being my friend and my business partner, then tell me now."

"I am comfortable being your partner and your friend. But nothing more," she said.

"Of course," he said kissing her lightly on the lips.

Caroline swatted him away. "You are so bad," she chided.

Caroline had had fun for the first time in a very long time. It might have been the wine or the ambience of the fresh air and the sound of the rushing river. She knew that the biggest thrill of all was discovering that a younger, handsome Italian man found her alluring.

Chapter Thirty-Five

Police Headquarters in Cagliari

After giving it much thought Caroline made the decision to file a formal complaint with the authorities against Julia. She felt that she had enough evidence to prove Julia's attempts on her life. She figured that the best-case scenario was that they would take her claims seriously and if they did not, they would be on the record. Caroline carried an Italian passport and was an Italian citizen through her birthright.

The room was warm and even with the windows cracked open, the air was still and clammy. She tossed and turned until the rooster crowed, and the morning light crept into the room. Caroline knew from previous sleepless nights, that in the dark everything looked bleak and daunting but as soon as the day dawned, things didn't seem so hopeless. She decided to get up and dress before the family were aware that she had left the house. They didn't take her accusations seriously and it was better that they did not know of her intentions.

Caroline took the early train to the main police headquarters in Cagliari. She wore a simple silk blouse with a pair of beige linen pants. Caroline did not dress like a tourist, she dressed like an Italian woman, elegant and with class. It was normal for strangers to speak to her in Italian, and although her Italian was good it was not perfect.

A young girl in her early twenties sat directly across from Caroline on the train. She smiled. "I like your bag?" she said. "That blue shade is so pretty."

"Thank you," said Caroline.

"Is it a Bottega Veneta?"

"Yes, it is. I bought it here, but I live in the United States." Caroline was used to Italians striking up a friendly conversation. This was not as common in Florida where people seemed to be more cautious of strangers.

"Where in the States do you live?" said the woman.

"I live in Miami, Florida."

"I have been there. A few years ago, I was an *au pair* for a family in Miami."

"That's great. Did you have a good experience?"

She uncrossed her legs and had to think about it. "I did. I liked my host family and the children very much, but I wasn't very happy there."

"Oh. Why not?"

"I found that everyone works too hard, and they don't make time to enjoy their lives," she said. She undid her ponytail and gathered her hair, twisting it into a messy bun. "I can't speak for the whole of America, but the people seem very materialistic. They keep buying more and more things, then have to work harder to pay for the stuff. Like a better car, a bigger house, fancy clothing labels."

"You don't find that here?"

"People like nice things here too but they are not obsessed. We work but we also have more time for the family. We take longer vacations. Our workplaces encourage that."

"That is true," Caroline said.

"But I did enjoy other things," she said. "Getting things done is much quicker. If you need any official business, it goes very quickly. Not like here, things can take days, weeks, months." She laughed. "Are you going shopping in Cagliari?"

"No, I'm going there on an official matter." Caroline looked out the window. "That's a pretty field," she said, trying to change the subject.

"May I ask what official business?"

Caroline cleared her throat; she wasn't sure if she wanted to tell her. Then she said, "I'm going to the police station to report an incident."

"The police? Are you kidding." She smiled brightly. "That's the kind of place where you will have a lot of delays," she said. "Good luck. You will need a lot of patience. Be strong, don't let them fob you off."

"I will try my best," Caroline said. "I am firm and obstinate." She smiled. "I guess you would say I am a pushy American."

They arrived at the train station at Cagliari. "*Buona fortuna!* good luck!" the girl called out as they got off the train.

Caroline checked her GPS on her phone for the *stazioni di polizia and* estimated it was about a ten-minute walk. She followed the directions until she arrived at her destination. As she approached the glass double-doors her heart was beating so fast that she had to stop and collect herself. She breathed in and out methodically. Be *firm and confident,* she told herself. With trembling hands, she pushed open the big glass door and walked inside. Caroline approached the officer sitting behind a glass partition at the front desk. The woman was concentrating on her computer, she briefly looked up. "Can I help you?" she asked.

"I would like to talk to a police officer," Caroline said.

The woman pointed to a clipboard on the ledge. "Fill out your name, address and phone number, please," she said. "Have a seat over there." She pointed to the waiting room.

Caroline took a seat and saw that she was the only one in the waiting room. It was bare except for the chairs and posters on the wall of wanted criminals. It felt like a prison but with open doors. A feeling of despair hung like a fog over the room. Caroline heard a tapping sound and realized it was her leg making that noise. A very tall, thin officer with a hunched posture came into the room.

"How can I help you?" he asked Caroline.

He had a wandering eye, and Caroline wasn't sure which eye to look at. "I have an issue that I need to discuss. I want to file a complaint," she said.

He sighed as if he had heard this request many times before.

"Follow me, Signora," he said.

He led her into a small office. He sat down at a desk, scratched his head and pointed with his chin to the empty seat in front of him. "Sit there. Tell me what your complaint is."

"I am an Italian citizen," she began, "but I live in the United States. I am visiting my family in Oristano. I came with my stepdaughter. Her father, my husband, is deceased. I thought that we got along but since my husband died there have been issues concerning his will."

"Signora, get to the point," he said.

Caroline took a deep breath. "My stepdaughter is attempting to kill me," she croaked.

"Excuse me?"

"She is trying to get rid of me, like murder me. I have pictures and proof."

"Let me get this straight. You want to file a police report that a family member is trying to kill you?"

"Yes. Here are the photos I have of what she has done." Caroline pulled up the images on her cell phone. "Can I show you them?"

He yawned and nodded. She stood up and went to his side of the desk. "This here is when she tried to drown me." She pointed to a photo of her lying on her stomach on the boat deck with the crew member hitting her on the back. The next photo was of water pouring out of her mouth. "This is when she attempted to poison me. Here is a photo of her bag with a bottle of anti-freeze in it. It is bright yellow, and as you can see, my vomit was bright yellow." She pointed to the next image. "I am in the hospital here, and there is a medical report."

The officer appeared to be writing things down on a pad but when Caroline looked over, he was doodling daisies and hearts.

"This photo is of my arm after she stabbed me in a restaurant. There are witnesses and also a hospital report."

The officer waved for her to sit back down. He put elbows on his desk and rested his chin in his hands. He leaned forward. "Why would this person, your daughter…"

"*Figliastra*, stepdaughter."

"Want to kill you?"

"My dead husband's trust dictates that all his assets and his money are left for my use until I die. What is left goes to his daughter." She looked at his left eye, then changed to the right eye. "Do you get it? Do you understand?" she pleaded.

"Signora. I get it. It could be a case, or it couldn't be a case. Sometimes what seems like it is, is not what it seems." He put his head in his hands and looked like he had the weight of the world on his shoulders. "Understand?"

"But I have the evidence. I have the proof," Caroline insisted. "She also left a dead cat on my bed. I have a photo. The other photos are absolute proof. She may even have her DNA on that anti-freeze bottle. That would be damning," Caroline said.

He abruptly stood up. "Write down your stepdaughter's full name, date of birth and address," he said, passing a sheet of paper to Caroline. "I have heard all you had to say. I have made a note of the important facts. You can file the report for attempted murder, but I must tell you that more incriminating evidence will be required to move forward," he said. "This girl is an American citizen, correct?"

"Yes."

"That may be a problem," he said. "I will give this report to my supervisor and await his comments. I will call you back in about two weeks and give you an update of the status of the complaint." He looked at his watch. "Oh, it's time for my lunch. Today my wife packed her specialty for me, pasta fagioli." He kissed his fingers to convey how delicious it was and ushered Caroline quickly out the door.

Chapter Thirty-Six

Julia and James

Julia lay on the bed in the hotel room with her head propped on pillows against the headboard. She balanced a tray on her stomach holding a cappuccino and a croissant. James had just come out of the shower. He was naked except for a towel wrapped around his waist. He held his phone in one hand and ran the other hand through his damp hair. Julia still was taken aback how attractive he was. She sometimes forgot.

"What are we going to tell Pia?" Julia asked. She dipped a piece of her croissant into a little pot of strawberry jam and took a bite.

"The truth. We will tell her that we don't have the money to pay her. Who knew that Caroline's ring was a friggin' fake?" he said.

"How were we to know that the bitch was wearing a replica diamond? It looked identical to the real one."

"We made fools of ourselves. We instruct Luca to steal Caroline's ring and then his contact comes back with the news that it's a cubic zirconia. In the meantime, Pia is waiting to be paid."

"This is a nightmare," Julia said. "The value of the real ring was over $100K. Are you going to call Pia? Maybe we should break the bad news in segments, like stall her for a bit." Julia took a sip of her coffee; her hand shook as she lifted the cup to her mouth and coffee splashed into the saucer.

"Pia told me that from the moment Caroline walked into her hair salon, she didn't like her," James added. "She had heard from Adela how Caroline got all the money from your father's estate that should have been yours."

"Well, Pia is Adela's best friend, she's a good person and she wants to help us."

"It's only for the money," James said.

"Now we can't even pay her. I feel terrible that we have put her in this position."

"Why don't you call her then?" he asked.

"Can't you see that I am eating my breakfast? I am starving."

"Julia this was your idea, remember? I warned you it could end up a big mess."

"Don't put the blame on me James," she seethed. "You agreed to everything. Don't forget that you are a crucial part of the team."

"Okay, okay, calm down." James sat on the floral upholstered chair by the writing desk and punched numbers into his phone. He put the call on speakerphone. "Hello Pia, it's me, can you talk?

"No. I am at work, I'm busy with a customer."

"Call me back as soon as you can."

"Is everything alright?"

"Um, nothing to worry about. There is a hiccup."

"What does that mean?"

"A little problem. I will explain later." He hung up.

Julia put the tray down on the floor. "We aren't going to be able to return to the States as planned." She sobbed. "I can't believe this is happening."

James came over and sat on the bed and put his arms around her. "I will find a solution. I always do." He kissed her on her forehead. "We will work out how to get the money. Where there's a will there's a way. You know that's my motto."

"This is harder for me, than for you," Julia said.

"I know."

"Pia is pregnant with our baby, and now we don't have the means to pay her like we promised."

Chapter Thirty-Seven

Lies

Giorgio sat at his desk and tapped his pen on a notepad. "Let's head storm to find a place to shoot our commercials."

"Brainstorm," Caroline corrected. She sat opposite him in his small office across from the laboratory.

"What?" he asked. "Think about a place that is classy and elegant. Like you."

"A resort or a spa?" Caroline suggested. Her arm had healed from where Julia had almost stabbed her. She was now ready to be the skincare spokesperson for the commercial.

Giorgio had hired an advertising agency to do the filming.

"If we can come up with a venue where we don't have to pay from our pockets, it will help with the budget."

"Did the bank get back to you about the loan?" Julia asked.

Giorgio ran his hand through his hair and looked defeated. "I heard from them yesterday. They turned us down. A courier dropped off their letter. Cowards – they didn't even call."

"Oh no! Why?"

"Something about not understanding the skincare business so they were not confident to go forward."

"What are we going to do? We don't have enough funds to finance this project," said Caroline.

"*Stai calmo*, keep calm," he said. "The amount of money that you and I will invest will be enough to launch the campaign. I am confident that as soon as we can prove that our sales are successful, they will change their minds and come through with financial support."

Giorgio stood up and opened the mini bar behind him. He took out a bottle of Veuve Clicquot, opened it with a pop, and poured it into two champagne glasses. He handed one to Caroline. He lifted his glass. "To a successful partnership," he said, clinking his glass against Caroline's. "Trust me," he added.

Caroline took a sip and shifted in her seat. She wasn't sure that she that this was a good idea, but she said, "My aunt and uncle have a yacht. That would be a perfect setting."

"Wonderful. A yacht is always a good backdrop for a luxury product. Who are you uncle and aunt?"

"The Accadis, from Costa Esmeralda."

"Beppe Accadi?" Giorgio perked up. "That's your uncle? He is a legend. I love that man. He has the biggest boat in Sardinia – that would be the perfect venue."

"I can ask him. Unfortunately, he and my aunt are having marital problems, so I don't know if he will want the exposure right now."

"He certainly is a ladies' man," said Giorgio. "I think he has slept with half of Sardinia."

Caroline felt irritated. *Who was he to point fingers at anyone being a womanizer?* "My aunt is having a very rough time right now. I'm doing my best to support her emotionally."

"You would think your aunt would be used to his screwing around after all these years," Giorgio commented.

"That's really not a nice thing to say," Caroline retorted.

Giorgio held up his hands like he was about to be shot. "I'm only joking," he said. "I know your aunt – she is a classy and elegant woman."

"Is that how you refer to all the women you want to impress?" Caroline blurted out. "I'm such a classy and elegant woman, remember?"

"Caroline, what is this? I think you are the best. Excuse me but my English is not so good. I don't have all the words to describe things. I would tell you that you are sexy but then you will be angry with me."

Giorgio's phone vibrated on his desk. It must have been turned to silent. The vibration on the glass sounded like a dentist's drill. "My wife," he said and grabbed the phone. He left the office to talk in private.

Caroline looked at Giorgio's desk; it was a mess. Piles of papers, letters, and forms were stacked in messy rows. There didn't seem to be any order. On the top of one pile, Caroline noticed a letter with the bank's bright blue letterhead. It was the same bank they had been dealing with about the loan. She could hear Giorgio talking on the phone, explaining why he wouldn't be back in time for dinner. Caroline quickly read the letter, and the first paragraph made her gasp. 'We are pleased to inform you that your loan for Glassique Skincare S.r.l has been approved.' Approved? Why had Giorgio lied? Blood rushed to her face, and she felt hot and dizzy. She jumped up and took a screenshot of the page.

"Bianca called to ask if I would be back at the restaurant for dinner," Giorgio announced as he walked into the office. He stopped in his tracks. "Why do you look so upset?"

"You don't have to be worried about my wife," he said. "I told you that she is happy we are doing this together. She agrees that you are a smart woman."

"I needed some air, so I was trying to open the window."

"Let me do it," he said. He opened the window. "See, It's really easy."

"Thank you. My hands are sticky. Why would you think that I am worried about your wife?" Caroline croaked.

"Because you look troubled," he said squeezing her hand.

Caroline pulled her hand away and stood up. "Ciao," she said, "I have to get back." She pushed past him.

"I'll give you a ride back home." Giorgio grabbed his car keys.

"No, no, I'd rather take a taxi."

She saw Giorgio scratching his head and looking puzzled as she bolted out the door.

"Don't forget to ask Beppe about the yacht," he called out after her.

Chapter Thirty-Eight

Beppe Has Gone to The Dogs

Caroline asked Ornella for permission to visit Beppe and to ask him if they could use the yacht as a backdrop for the filming of the skincare commercial.

"He has moved in with his whore," Ornella announced on the phone. She took a shaky breath. "Into her small, run-down apartment with two children climbing all over the place." She knew the situation because she had sent one of her own cleaning ladies over to get a detailed account of what went on there. "My husband, who was a king at home, is now living like a pauper," she said.

"I really can't imagine Uncle Beppe living in such dire circumstances," Caroline said. "Are you sure that you are okay with me using the boat?"

"Of course. It's my yacht. He bought it for me for my sixtieth birthday." She cleared her throat, and her voice cracked. "Besides, you can report back to me about what's going on."

Caroline could hear the dogs barking in the background.

"They are crying," Ornella sniffed. "They miss their daddy, but I refuse to let them go and visit him in that hellhole. They would be traumatized. That is not a good environment for them – the psychologist said so."

Caroline found the apartment building where Beppe was staying with Laura. She found Laura's name on the board and pressed the buzzer.

"Who's there?" answered Beppe, in a feeble voice.

"It's me, Caroline. Can I come up?"

He buzzed her through the large wooden doors. There wasn't an elevator, so Caroline walked up the three flights of stairs and knocked on the door. An old gray-haired man opened it timidly. "Uncle Beppe?" she asked, stunned. She hardly recognized him.

"Come in, come in," he said.

Beppe offered Caroline a beverage, but she declined.

"Uncle how are you holding up?" she asked.

Beppe was slumped in the chair. "I'm doing fine," he said.

"Excuse my boldness," Caroline said, "but you don't look like you are."

"When you find true love all your needs change," he said, sounding unconvinced.

"Is Laura here?" she asked.

"She has gone to pick up the children from school." He rubbed his chin as if debating whether to tell Caroline. He burst into tears.

"Uncle, what's the matter?"

"I miss my doggies," he cried. "Ornella won't let me see them." He put his head in his hands and his body heaved as he sobbed.

Caroline jumped up and put her arms around him. A wave of pity rushed over her.

"I'm sure you and aunty will come to a resolution. The attorneys will find a way."

Beppe wiped his tears on his sleeve and held out his hand. "A tissue," he said.

Caroline scrambled in her bag and retrieved a crumpled napkin from Mama Sophia's restaurant. She handed it to him. When he recognized the name of the place, he sobbed even more loudly.

"I miss my home," he cried. "I want to go home." He blew his nose so hard that the chandelier shook.

The room became silent. Beppe realized what he had said and was stunned. He had shocked himself by saying out loud what he really wanted. Just then the sound of squealing children grew louder until the door opened.

Beppe shot up straight in his chair, wiped his eyes, and whispered to Caroline, "I am too old for this."

Laura bounced in and stopped in her tracks when she saw Caroline. "What is she doing here?" she turned to ask Beppe.

"I came to ask my uncle if I can film a commercial on his boat," Caroline answered.

"You could have called," Laura said. She avoided eye contact.

The children, a girl and a boy, both under ten years old, jumped on Beppe's lap and threw their arms around his neck. He patted them on the head dismissively until they hopped off.

Laura stood to his side with her arms folded and gave Caroline a look that said *you are not welcome here.* Caroline was surprised to see how ordinary she looked, unlike the women he usually chased. Laura was petite and non-descript. Her brown hair was pulled off her face in a messy bun, she was make-up free except for a smear of clear lip gloss. She wore a drab t shirt and matching cargo pants. Laura looked younger than her years, a mother of two--yet she looked like a teenager. Beppe could have been her grandfather. In spite of looking younger than her age, she exuded confidence that she demonstrated by sidling up to Beppe, massaging his shoulders, and kissing the top of his head.

"Amore, can I get you something to eat?" she asked.

"I already had something," he said. He pulled away from her.

Laura looked affronted. "I hope your niece hasn't upset you," she said. "You are not acting like yourself. Why are your eyes so swollen? Is anything wrong?"

"Your boyfriend misses his dogs," Caroline piped up.

"You mean my fiancé," Laura corrected. She cocked her head to the side. "Is that true, Beppe?"

"Yes," he said, without enthusiasm. "The truth is that I miss Remy and Lily terribly."

The children perked up. "We want to see Remy and Lily," they cried.

"I've told you a hundred times that the dogs can visit you here. It's not my fault that the bitch won't allow it," Laura said.

Beppe looked defeated. "I understand that. That doesn't mean that I don't long for my puppies." He turned towards Laura. "Please don't call my wife a bitch, after all she is the mother of my doggies."

Laura ran out of the room holding back tears. "I can't believe you said that. Get real Beppe, they are just bloody dogs, not children," she called out through her sobs.

Caroline stood up. "Okay then, I have to get going," she said. She buttoned up her cardigan and picked up her bag from the floor. "So, I can use your boat?" she asked Beppe.

"Yes, yes," he muttered. "You can have the boat for all I care. Nothing matters to me anymore.

"Even the dogs?" Caroline chided.

"Only the dogs," he said firmly. "I have made up my mind. I don't want to live without my dogs."

Chapter Thirty-Nine

Conception

Pia sat on the armchair in the hotel room bent over, crying. "You promised me the money. That's what I did this for," she said. "I shouldn't have trusted you both. I should have asked for the money upfront. Now it's too late. I'm pregnant."

"Pia, we will get the money, just be patient. We didn't think for one second that the ring was fake," James said.

Julia went over to Pia and put her arms around her. Pia shrugged her off.

"I blame myself for being so stupid," Pia said. "Nothing is in writing. Surrogacy is illegal here. I was trying to help you guys out. You wanted a baby, and I can give you that." Pia straightened up and shot them an angry look. "But I'm not Mother Theresa, I want compensation for this, and you better give me what you promised."

"I told you we will get the money. It has to be in cash so there is no trail and it's not easy to get $100,000 in cash," James said.

Pia cocked her head to the side. "What about the plane fare and all the expenses you need to cover for me in Florida?" she said. "Am I still going as planned?"

"Pia, stop worrying. James told you that we will come up with something. We just need a bit of time," Julia said, firmly.

Julia was furious with James, but she couldn't let Pia know her true feelings. It was he who came up with the idea a few weeks before Julia left with her stepmother to Sardinia. James had concocted a scheme that he thought was the best chance for them to have a baby. He had planned to also go to Sardinia and hide out in a hotel close by.

James had never met Adela's husband Luca but had spoken to him on the phone. He felt that Luca would be a good contact to help him, and Julia find a way for them to have a baby. James had explained their predicament, that Julia could not carry a child, and asked Luca if he knew of a woman in Sardinia who would be willing to be a surrogate for them. Luca had researched and told James that surrogacy was illegal in Italy. That had squashed that idea. However, a few days later, Luca called to say that he had a better idea. He knew of a woman who would be willing to carry their baby, for a price.

James had to first get consent from Julia. They were having breakfast some weeks before when James had brought up the subject. "I have a plan for a baby for us," he said to Julia.

"You do?" she asked, without enthusiasm.

"Luca knows a young woman who is open to carrying our baby for us."

"What's the catch?"

"Because surrogacy isn't legal in Italy, she will have to conceive using my sperm and then fly to the States and have the baby there. Then we will legally adopt the child."

"What about my egg? How will you retrieve my egg."

"That's the tricky part. We have to do this ourselves. There cannot have any medical intervention involved." James cleared his throat and said, "We will have to use her egg and my sperm."

Julia looked at her husband in disbelief. "Are you kidding me?" she said, affronted. "So, what you are telling me is that the baby will be genetically yours but not mine?"

"Think about it, babe." He rubbed his nose and didn't make eye contact. "Your eggs were tested, and they were not viable. This is the best solution for us. You will adopt the baby, and it will be 100% yours."

"I don't think so!" Julia hurled her brush at him.

James ducked. "You don't want to carry a child, remember? You don't want to ruin your figure. I don't think that there are that many options out there, except adoption. Which would be fine. But like this, the baby will at least have my genes."

"Who is this woman?"

"A good friend of Adela's and Luca. She is a hairdresser in their town."

"Why would she be willing to do this?"

"Obviously for the money, but maybe she wants to help a couple have a child."

"Please James." She rolled her eyes. "Don't be so naïve."

"We will have to pay her in cash – that is her stipulation," James said.

"Okay, it's definitely for the money, but I suppose what difference does it make to us? How do you intend to get $100,000 in cash? In a foreign country?"

James coughed. He picked up a bottle of water and took a sip. "You know that enormous diamond ring that Caroline wears?" he said, "don't ask me for details, but Luca can sell it on the underground market in Sardinia."

Julia took a shaky breath and shook her head. "That is insane. Someone is going to steal Caroline's ring. This is getting more complicated by the minute," she said.

"You haven't heard the biggest complication of all. I don't like it, and you are not going to either."

"What next?"

"I will have to have sex with this woman."

"You are kidding, right?"

"Seriously, we are not doing this in a clinic. We will be doing this in my hotel room. I will have to impregnate her."

"What about a turkey baster?"

"What are you smoking? Those don't work in real life."

Julia wasn't certain that James was right about that; she had a chilling feeling that he might be lying to her. But she pushed the thought aside. She wanted a baby too, after all.

"I don't know if I can go through with this," Julia said. "This is a whole different level. Now my husband has to have sex with a strange woman." She paced back and forth and stopped in front of the full-length mirror. "Am I dreaming?" she asked her reflection. "James, it's not that simple to conceive, we know, we have been trying for so long. This girl… what's her name?

"Pia."

"She has to be ovulating at the time of conception. It's all about the right timing," Julia said.

"I know. She is already tracking her cycle with a home kit to see when she will be ovulating."

"Wow, James. Thanks for telling me. All this was going on behind my back."

"I know you are a worrier," he said. "I didn't want to burden you with all the details."

"I don't know if I can go through with this." She shook her head.

"I don't know if I can go through this either," he said. "Luca texted me a picture of this girl, a heifer would be a kind description."

"That's not good," Julia said. "We want a nice-looking baby."

"She is naturally blonde and has a pretty face if that makes you feel any better."

"I have to think about this," said Julia. "I want a baby, but I didn't expect that my husband would have to be an active participant. This is going to be like a military operation. I will be in Oristano and so will you. We will have to pretend that you are in Florida. Caroline's family must not know about this. They would put a stop to it."

James rubbed at the slight stubble on his chin. "It's not going to be easy. We want a baby, so we will have to do this. I will stay at a hotel close by. We will Facetime and pretend that I am back at home." James took his wife's hands in his. "We will have to wait for the money from the diamond, then we can proceed with the implantation."

A crease formed between Julia's brows. "Let's tell it like it is. We are going to steal my stepmother's ring, sell it and use the money to illegally impregnate a strange woman, take her to America, wait for her to give birth, then adopt the baby." Julia stood up and put her face close to her husband's. "It's so simple, what can go wrong?" she asked.

"Babe, sometimes in life one has to do things to get the things that you want. Caroline has stiffed you out of your father's money. You asked her for the money for a surrogate in the States and she refused. So, what is the alternative?"

"You are right. I leave in two weeks with her for Sardinia. Book your flight."

James beamed. "It's a plan," he said, kissing her lightly on the lips.

Julia managed to smile. "We've got to do what we got to do," she said.

James and Pia had to co-ordinate the time of the month when she would be ovulating. They had sex three times in three days. Julia sat in the lounge connected to the bedroom in the hotel suite. She blocked her ears with her fingers not to hear any sounds from the copulating couple.

Pia wore a cotton nightgown that she lifted for the penetration. James had reassured Julia that he did not find Pia sexually arousing and had to think of his wife the entire time. After two weeks, Pia took a pregnancy test, and it was positive. According to the oral agreement she now had to be paid. They would have to come up with the money fast or she threatened to go to a neighboring country and have an abortion.

Chapter Forty

The Photoshoot

Caroline sucked in her breath between clenched jaws. "Please be gentle," she told Bianca as Bianca applied the truffle moisturizer to Caroline's face with jerky movements.

Caroline was having her make-up and hair done in a cabin on the yacht for the skincare shoot. Giorgio's wife, Bianca, was the make-up artist.

"Has she done this before?" Caroline asked Giorgio.

"Yes, yes," he assured her. "Bianca was a model, and she also did hair and make-up."

But Caroline was skeptical when Bianca worked on her. When she applied the foundation with a brush, she gripped Caroline's chin too fiercely. When she applied coats of mascara, she used aggressive movements that dipped the wand accidently into her eye.

"Ouch," Caroline said. "My eye is stinging. Please be careful."

"*La bellezze e dolore*, beauty is pain," said Bianca. "Did your mother never tell you that?"

When the makeover was finished, Caroline was not happy. She looked over-done, like a used-up hooker. Her eyes were too dark, her cheeks too red, and her lipstick too exaggerated. A young man teased her blonde hair out like a dandelion. Caroline swore that she saw him wink at Bianca.

Caroline called Giorgio aside. "I am supposed to look chic and elegant," she said. "I look like a clown."

Giorgio nodded. He asked his wife, "Darling, can you make her look more natural?"

"No," Bianca answered. She took a long draw on her cigarette, then blew out the smoke in a perfect circle. "This woman is not naturally pretty. I had to contour her face to hide her faults. That takes skill."

"I don't like it," Caroline whispered to Giorgio.

Bianca turned abruptly to face Caroline. "I am not a magician," she said. She took a bunch of make-up wipes and scrubbed off her work with harsh strokes. She threw the wipes in a trash can and stormed off.

Caroline's face was red and swollen. She reapplied her make-up with a shaking hand, she battled to draw the eyeliner uniformly. Caroline then wet her hair with a spray bottle and blow-dried it with a round brush. She checked her skin so that it looked smooth and unlined, after all —the skincare products promised glassy skin.

"That's much better," said Giorgio.

"I don't think that your wife likes me," Caroline said.

"I apologize; it was a misunderstanding. I thought my wife knew what she was doing."

"I heard that!" Bianca shouted from the galley. "I am sick and tired of placating the women you choose to scam."

Only the sounds of the waves lapping on the sides of the boat broke the silence.

"What does she mean?" Caroline asked. "Why did she say you are scamming me?"

Caroline reclined on the white sofa against a pile of plush cushions. While the photographer shot the photos, her smile froze into a grimace.

"Pay no attention. My wife is talking nonsense. Just stick to the script and let's get this done," said Giorgio.

Caroline extolled the virtues of the Glassique serum in a calm and professional manner but deep inside she was trembling. She felt something was not right. A few days before she had gone with Giorgio to the bank and transferred a large amount of money from her bank account into his. She had paid no attention to her family's warning. Was Bianca, right? Was Giorgio conning her?

Bianca pulled her hairdresser friend by the hand. "I've had enough of this *stronzata*, bullshit," she said, "let's get the hell out of here."

As they made their way off the boat, Beppe and Ornella, each carrying a miniature Yorkie, ascended the gangway.

As soon as Caroline finished filming, they ran up to her and gave her a hug.

"We have good news," Beppe announced.

"What is the good news?" asked Caroline. She had guessed what it was.

"My beloved queen and I are back together."

"That's wonderful!" Caroline exclaimed.

"Let's be real," corrected Ornella. "My husband is only back with his beloved *queen* for one reason –the dogs."

"Not true," Beppe said, "I missed you and I missed the dogs."

"I know you came back because of the puppies. I'm fine with that. Just be honest with me for a change," Ornella said.

"I am so happy for you both," Caroline said.

"It cost me a lot to end it with Laura," he said, rubbing his fingers together as the universal sign of money. "But it is worth it. I have my family back." He bent forward to kiss his wife on the cheek, but she pulled away.

"I am too old for this nonsense," she said. "I threw out all his purple pills. The man can't get it up anymore, so let's hope he will settle down with me. After forty-five years it's about time.

They sat down to lunch on the back deck under a white canopy. Giorgio sat next to Caroline. She stood up and moved to the other side. The table was set with a red and white striped tablecloth. A line of fresh pomegranates ran down the center of the table and lemons tumbled out of a huge wooden bowl. Large red goblets added a touch of nobility. Everything that Ornella did was with an artistic flair. Beppe admired that. He was a man who appreciated the finer things in life. He had never known how important that was to him until he moved in with his mistress, Laura. Her home was messy and the children loud. She didn't know how to cook. Laura was young and pretty, but she lacked taste in her clothes. The sex may have lured him for a while but for a man like Beppe that was never enough. He soon became bored.

Beppe sat at the head of the table looking out to the ocean. He raised his glass in a toast. "Salute!" he called out. Beppe was a content man, for that moment. He was happy to be back home.

Chapter Forty-One

When Push Comes to Shove

Caroline woke up early that morning, jumped out of bed, drank a coffee and was out the door before she could change her mind. She had had an epiphany during the night. She would go straight to the hotel where she knew that Julia and James were hiding out and confront them. Why was James in Oristano? Why had they stolen her ring? She had so many questions and before they left Sardinia, she wanted to get some answers.

Caroline knew exactly where they were staying. A few days ago, Salvatore had finally told her the development that he had been saving for the right time. He was concerned that James and Julia would leave Sardinia in the next few days.

Caroline strode along the cobbled streets straight to the brown brick hotel down the small alleyway. The doorman opened the large wooden door for Caroline without hesitation. She looked like she belonged and knew where she was going. Always immaculately dressed, Caroline could pass for any upper-class Italian woman. The gods were on her side. The young lady sitting at the front desk was arguing on the phone and glanced up at Caroline waiving her to the elevator. The elevator, an old wooden crate with brass buttons and a folding gate, looked like the original one from a century ago.

Caroline knocked three times on the door of the hotel suite. She knew the room number. She heard the clicking of heels approach the door.

"Who is it?" Julia asked, in English.

"Housekeeping," she answered.

The door opened and when Julia saw who it was, she tried to immediately shut it. "James!" she called out in a shaky voice. "What is she doing here?"

Caroline pushed open the door and barged inside. James's mouth hit the floor. "Get out," he said. "I'm calling security."

Caroline pushed past Julia and stood firmly with her hands on her hips. "Go ahead," she said. "I have proof that you stole my ring, took it to a dealer and discovered it was fake. I filed a police report with the dealer's statement."

"How dare you come here," James said. "We will arrest you for trespassing."

"Oh really?" Caroline said. "The only ones who will be arrested are the two of you. I filed a police investigation against the two of you."

"That's such bullshit, Caroline. What for?"

"That you are both conspiring to kill me."

James burst out laughing. "Are you for real? They will see that you are a nut job."

"I have all the proof I need. Every time Julia tried but failed to kill me, I documented and photographed everything.

"Bullshit," Julia piped up. "Why would we want to kill you? Do you really think that you are so important to us that we would risk our lives? Besides why would the Italian police ever believe you, an American?" she scoffed.

"I am an Italian citizen," said Caroline. "Did you forget that I was born here? They are taking this very seriously."

"You are full of crap, Caroline. Why would I even want to kill you?"

"Money."

"The only time I ever asked you for money was to pay for a surrogate to carry a child for us. Of course you turned us down. But you are delusional to think that I would murder you for that?"

Caroline stepped towards the min- bar, took out a bottle of water, opened the cap and took a sip. "How did you think that you could steal my ring and get away with it."

"We are desperate." James raked his fingers through his hair and bit his lip.

"We found a suitable woman to carry our baby. She is now pregnant, and we promised her the money and now we can't pay her."

"That not my problem," Caroline said. "Why are you so frantic to pay her? You both have tons of money." She turned to James. "I know what you make, it's a fortune for what you do. I see the statements, remember?"

"Gambling," Julia said. She looked at James furiously. "He gambles online and that's where our money has gone."

"Well, then you are an idiot James, and it's not my problem."

"We don't have anything. It's a façade," said Julia. Her bottom lip trembled.

"So, you came up with a plan to kill me so you could get your father's money sooner. Do you think I don't know that?"

"You are delusional, Caroline, we may be selfish, but we aren't killers. This isn't a thriller movie."

"Well, you will have to tell that to a judge."

Julia walked towards Caroline with tears in her eyes. "I beg of you. Will you please give us the money to cover the pregnancy and birth? The surrogate has medical expenses, and she will have to have the baby in the States because it's not legal here."

"Don't cry your crocodile tears to me." Caroline turned to walk out the door.

Julia jumped up and barred her way. "I'm begging you Caroline, what else do you want me to do?"

Caroline pushed past Julia and walked out of the room. Julia followed.

Caroline pressed the elevator button. Julia grabbed onto her jacket sleeve. "I promise I won't ever ask you for money again," she pleaded.

The elevator arrived but stopped short of the floor. Caroline pushed the steel gates open, there was a drop under the elevator cage. Caroline was about to step into the carriage. She felt a shove, losing her grip, she went tumbling down. Her screams echoed throughout the building.

"I didn't do it!" Julia screamed. "I didn't push her."

James ran towards the elevator. "What happened?" he shouted. He looked wild eyed at his wife. "Did you push her?" he mouthed.

The security guard called the ambulance. In one minute, the medics arrived, followed by the police and the fire department.

"I didn't push her," Julia kept repeating. "She fell. It was an accident."

They took Caroline away on a gurney. When she arrived at the hospital, she was in shock. Her breath was shallow, and she couldn't speak. The doctors told Rosalia that it was a miracle. She had only fallen one floor and for that reason she had made it out alive.

The police took Julia to the precinct for questioning. They had the report that Caroline had filed previously about the knife attack. They held Julia in jail until the issue was resolved.

Chapter Forty-Two

The Hospital

Salvatore knew the Chief of Police very well. In fact, he was his cousin. After the last attempt on Caroline's life, Salvatore and Rosalia paid him a visit to his home. Ernesto Gambino the chief of police in Cagliari was a big man who kept his inner feelings to himself. When Salvatore filled him in on what was going on between Caroline and her stepdaughter, he listened intently but remained expressionless.

It was his wife Constantina who was aghast. "This is terrible!" she exclaimed. "Poor Caroline, she has been through so much with the death of her husband and now this? Her monster stepdaughter, trying to kill her?"

The Chief of Police bit his bottom lip and squinted. He said, "*Tried* to kill her. She hasn't achieved her goal yet. There lies the difference."

"Signor Capo della Polizia," Rosalia said. "But for the grace of God, my niece isn't dead. There have been a number of serious attempts to end her life. We believe she is in danger."

"Thank goodness Caroline's mother isn't aware of what is going on," said Signora Gambino. "God works in mysterious ways, if she was of right mind, this would have killed her."

"Never mind her mother, what about her?" said Salvatore. "Caroline has to be protected at all times until this *donna malvagia*, wicked woman, and her husband, who is also involved, are in jail."

"I will place a guard outside her hospital room. That's all we can do for the moment. We will also interrogate the *la figliastra*, the stepdaughter, but we cannot hold her without evidence," Chief Gambino said, through a yawn.

Gambino made it very obvious that he was done with the conversation and ready for his Sunday afternoon nap.

As his wife ushered Rosalia and Salvatore out the door she assured them that she would not let him forget his promise. "Sometimes a wife can be very skillful when sharing a pillow with her husband." She winked.

The very next day an armed police officer was stationed around the clock outside Caroline's hospital room. Only immediate family, her aunts Rosalia and Ornella, were permitted to visit. Rosalia arrived with a bunch of freshly cut flowers from her garden and a container of *pastina*/chicken broth with pasta. She found Caroline sitting propped up against her pillows in bed feverishly writing in a notebook.

She looked up. "Hi Aunt. Please excuse the way I look. I am a mess."

Rosalia was surprised to see that Caroline looked much better than she expected. She was not covered in bandages and only had slight bruising on her arms.

"You look much better than I expected," Rosalia said.

"I am in a lot of pain, but the doctor told me that I was very fortunate that I broke the fall into the elevator."

"Not the shaft?"

"The elevator stopped between the floors and when Julia pushed me, fortunately I fell down into the elevator. Of course, Julia hoped that I would fall down the shaft and be killed."

Rosalia unwrapped the flowers and put them in a vase that she had brought with her. She had always thought that it was inconsiderate when people brought flowers without a container to put them in. Most places like a hospital or a hotel don't have vases readily available.

"What are you writing?" she asked her niece.

"The police asked me for a detailed report on all the methods Julia used to try and harm me. I wanted to write it all down before I forget."

"There is a police officer posted outside your door at all times," Rosalia reassured her. "You can relax – no one can harm you."

Caroline stretched her arms and winced. Rosalia could tell that she was in pain.

"Who would have thought that your visit to come and see me would end up being such a nightmare," Rosalia said.

"I really should never have brought Julia with me," Caroline said. "I thought I was doing something kind for her since her father died, I feel so stupid now."

"I was wrong to think that the two of you had a good relationship," said Rosalia, "I can now tell that from the beginning she was jealous of your relationship with her father."

Caroline took a spoon full of the soup. "It's so good," she said. "Did I tell you that I went to the hotel where Julia was staying with James."

"Salvatore told me that he discovered that James was in town." Rosalia scratched her forehead. "What is he doing here?"

"He has been in Oristano this whole time. He came to impregnate a woman, and if she conceived, which she did, they were going to pay her $100,000 to carry their baby."

"Are you kidding me?"

"You couldn't make this stuff up. James got Luca to steal my diamond ring and sell it on the black market. But guess what? I was too clever for them. I never travel with my real diamonds – it was an imitation."

Rosalia's mouth dropped open. "Why is Luca involved? Who is this girl?"

"Her name is Pia."

"Pia? Adela's best friend Pia?"

"I don't know who she is, but she agreed to carry Julia and James's baby. Surrogacy is illegal in Italy so the baby would have to be born in America."

"How does it help them if you are dead?" Rosalia said.

"Because Julia stands to get all the money that Stuart left, but as you know only after I die."

"James is an attorney, he has money. I don't understand why they are so desperate."

"I found out that they don't have money. He has a gambling addiction."

Rosalia shook her head. "The sooner you go back home, the better," she said.

"I am not going anywhere until I get Julia locked up. As long as she is free, I am a dead person walking. I always thought she was unstable, but I never thought that she was a psychopath. This has been a rude awakening."

Chapter Forty-Three

The Visitor

"Signora?" The police guard knocked lightly on Caroline's hospital room door.

"Yes?" Caroline answered. She had just finished eating her breakfast. Scrambled eggs on toast and watered-down coffee.

He opened the door. "There is a gentleman here who wishes to see you. He is not on your list, but he assured me that you will want to see him."

"Who is it?" Caroline asked. The only man that would want to see her was Giorgio. She had been expecting him to show up.

"Signor Giorgio Lanconi," the guard said.

"Hold on a minute," Caroline said. She opened the lid of the tray over her bed and looked in the mirror. Her hair stood up like a porcupine. She patted her hair down and raked her bangs straight with her fingers. Caroline was never too far from her lip-gloss, and it was in the same place where she had left it. She glossed the pink applicator over her dry lips, then smudged a trace of lip gloss over the apples of her cheeks. Giorgio walked in just as she slammed the vanity lid shut.

"My dearest, what has happened to you?" he asked. The creases in his forehead furrowed with concern.

"She did it again," Caroline said in a dead tone. "She tried to bump me off."

"My darling," Giorgio bent down and kissed her on the forehead. "You are a monkey with so many lives."

"It's a cat with nine lives, Giorgio."

"Yes… something like that." He sat down on the edge of the bed. "Your stepdaughter is dangerous." He bent over and brushed a loose strand of hair out of Caroline's eyes. "Don't you worry, I will protect you."

"I'm so lucky to have you protect me," Caroline said with a straight face.

"The reason I came is to tell you that I saw the reels of the commercial, and I have to say myself they are *magnifico!*"

"Magnificent?" Caroline repeated, "I am so glad."

His face turned serious. He inhaled and exhaled deeply. "The problem is that we don't have enough funds to go further. As you know the bank turned down the loan." Giorgio looked as though he was about to burst into tears. "Unless we come up with the money we can't go further," he said. He clapped his hands together with a big bang.

"Please Giorgio, I just took my pain meds," Caroline said. "I am feeling a little fuzzy. I can't concentrate right now."

"We have to launch as soon as we can so that everything is fresh in the potential buyers' minds," he said. "You know, strike while the oven is hot."

"It's the iron, Giorgio." She shook her head. "What do you want me to do?"

"Can you call your bank in the States and have them transfer funds to my account?"

"Okay" Caroline said. "How much?"

Giorgio seemed pleasantly surprised that she was agreeable to his suggestion. He adjusted his body language to accommodate the good news. He straightened up and with a confident voice, he said, "Excellent. Call now while it is still early enough to allow time for the transfer. Then he said we need $200,000 to cover all the expenses prior to launch."

"$200,000?" Caroline said.

"It's on a loan account," Giorgio said. He rubbed the palm of his hands on his jeans. "You will get it all back. We will have an attorney draw up the agreement."

Caroline sat silently. The only thing going through her mind was how Giorgio's English was so much better when it came to discussing money.

Caroline punched in the phone number of her financial institution. She immediately recognized the voice on the other end. She regularly made calls to her financial advisor to transfer funds in and out of her account.

"Hi Bruce," she said. "I'm in Italy. How are you? I'm doing okay, some minor hiccups but working through them.

I have a request. I need you to transfer $200,000 from my savings portfolio into an Italian bank account."

Caroline listened to the voice on the other line. "I understand. I'll wait. How long will it take to liquidate some of my stocks?"

She turned to Giorgio and mouthed, "Write down your bank account number and routing number."

Giorgio took out his check book from his leather satchel to get his banking information.

"Also, the pin. They need your pin to verify your account," she whispered.

With his half-rim glasses perched on the edge of his nose; Giorgio scrawled the numbers on a used paper bag. Caroline was taken aback by how much older he looked. Hunched over, he looked like an aging professor. Beads of sweat formed on his forehead and the tip of his tongue peeked out of his mouth while he was in deep concentration. When he was done, he handed the paper bag to Caroline.

She read the information out to her financial advisor. After she hung up the phone, she told Giorgio that the money would not transfer immediately because they had to sell some of her investments to get the cash.

If Giorgio was disappointed, he did not show it. "You just get better," he said, "that's the main thing."

Caroline didn't know if she was imagining things, but she thought she saw him do a little jig as he left the room.

Chapter Forty-Four

Two Friends

Ernesto Gambino, chief of police, was a little man with a big presence. What he lacked in height, he gained in confidence. His mind was always calculating the odds of any given situation. Caroline could tell right away that whatever she told him, he put in his memory bank if needed for later.

He looked cheerful when he approached the bed, but his eyes bored into hers seeking the truth. "Signora, you claim that Julia Callahan, daughter of your late husband Stuart Anderson is attempting to kill you. Is that correct?"

"Yes. That is correct," said Caroline. She adjusted the pillows behind her and sat up straighter.

"I believe you have forwarded evidence to corroborate your story, including DNA samples that still are being processed."

"Yes." Caroline took a sip of water from her cup. Although the scans and x-rays showed no bone breakages, she had scratches and bruising from her fall.

"You were very lucky that the elevator was stuck between floors," he said, "otherwise you would have fallen down the shaft and your injuries would have been graver, or you might have even died." He pursed his lips and let out a soft whistle. "You are a very lucky woman," he said, "three attempts on your life and you have survived. He looked up and pointed. "Someone up there is on your side."

"Are you going to arrest her?"

"We are building a case and then we will extradite your stepdaughter back to the States. She will be charged there."

"For what?"

"Attempted murder," he declared as if he said this on a daily basis. He drummed his fingers on her food tray and leaned over to inspect the wound on her forehead. He squinted at the clear strips of bandage that covered the stitches. "About six stitches," he said. "It could have been much worse."

"It is lucky I am alive," she said. "I think my late husband was watching over me."

Chief Gambino wrote some notes in his notebook. He still did things the old-fashioned way. He couldn't get used to using a laptop. As he left the hospital, he called Salvatore and asked him to meet him for an espresso at the local bar. By the time he walked to the café, Salvatore was already standing at a high-top table with two coffees.

"*Buongiorno amico mio*, Good morning my friend," the chief greeted him. "Let's sit down at a table," he continued, "I have a few questions for you."

They carried their coffees to a table and ordered a prosciutto sandwich to share. The two men had been friends since childhood and although Salvatore was older, they had lived in the same neighborhood and played street games together. Ernesto had been a small, puny boy with a speech impediment and whenever anyone bullied him, Salvatore, who was bigger and stronger, rushed to protect him. Ernesto had never forgotten that kindness and he had a soft spot for the older man.

Chief Gambino drank his espresso in one gulp followed by a sip of water. Then he bit into his sandwich and, with his mouth full, he said, "What motive would this girl Julia have to want to kill her stepmother?"

Salvatore answered, "Money. The root of all evil. I've been told by my wife that Caroline received the bulk of her husband's estate to use until she died."

"That's a common thing that husband's do," Ernesto said. "It's stupid in my opinion. Especially in a situation where the man has children from a prior marriage. It's human nature for them to wish that their father's wife would die so that they can get their money. But of course, no one in their right mind would try and murder the wife."

Salvatore took the last bite of his sandwich and brushed the remaining crumbs off his chin. "I have to say this Julia strikes me as a conniving type. Not only is she attempting to"—Salvatore ran his finger across his neck—"Caroline, but she and her husband are planning to have a baby using a local girl as the surrogate."

Ernesto was a man who had heard it all, and nothing surprised him, but this piqued his interest. He raised his eyebrows. "Tell me more," he said.

"Apparently Julia does not want to carry a child. To make a long story short, her husband James, has been here secretly having sex in a local hotel with this girl so that she can conceive. They are not using a doctor or any medical facility because as you know surrogacy is illegal here. From what I know, she did conceive and is going to fly back to the States with Julia and her husband, to have the baby born there."

The Chief shook his head. "*Non puoi inventare queste cose,* you can't make this stuff up," he said. He scratched his head. "Obviously she doesn't care that her husband is having sex with another woman. To top it all, she thinks that she will get away with murder, then go back home and raise a child happily ever after. What world do these people live in?"

"Do you have strong enough evidence to build a case?" asked Salvatore.

"Caroline has been clever. I am quite impressed," Chief Gambino said. "She has taken photos and kept a log with evidence of all the attempts against her life. Because Signora

Caroline is an Italian citizen, we were able to open a docket and submit the information to the USA. If they believe there is due cause, they will arrest Julia when she arrives on US soil."

"At the airport?"

"Yes." He looked directly at Salvatore. "My friend, this is confidential. Off the record. Do not discuss with anyone – even your wife."

"Naturally," Salvatore said. "What was supposed to be an enjoyable family reunion has turned into a circus."

"My life is always a circus," Ernesto chuckled. "My wife still can't understand why I don't like to talk to her after I get home. I'm drained from all the drama."

Chapter Forty-Five

Losers Never Win

There was a loud knock on the front door. Not the usual visitor type of knocking but an irritable, demanding knocking. Salvatore glanced at Rosalia. "I will get it," he said.

When he opened the door, Giorgio Lanconi stood like a bull ready to charge out the gate. "Where is she?" he asked, pushing past Salvatore.

"Good morning," said Salvatore. "Where are your manners?"

"It's not a good morning," Giorgio said. "Where is Signora Caroline?"

"Come in, come in," Salvatore said. He pointed to the sofa. "Sit down, take a deep breath. I will get Caroline."

Caroline was not expecting visitors. She was still recuperating after her fall. Her hair was in a messy bun, and she was still in her pajamas. Make-up free, she didn't look as perfect as usual. Giorgio didn't seem to notice.

"My money is gone," he blurted out. "All of it. The business account has been cleared out."

"I don't understand," Caroline said. She sat down opposite Giorgio.

"I checked my bank account this morning because I had to use some of the funds." He was breathing heavily and clasped his chest. "Zero balance. Zero. I thought there was a mistake. I went to the bank, and they confirmed that all the money had been withdrawn."

"Who took it?"

"My wife," he said.

"Bianca?"

"She's the only wife I have. Bianca is missing and the money has gone." He put his head in his hands and bent over. He rocked back and forth.

"Don't panic," Caroline said. "It could be a misunderstanding. Don't look at the worst-case scenario."

"Please don't be an idiot!" he yelled. "I have to pay for the equipment and supplies. What am I going to do?" He threw hands up into the air. "That was all the money you deposited for the business."

Rosalia heard the commotion and came into the room. "I have fresh orange juice and biscotti for both of you," she said. She set the tray down on the side table. "Buongiorno Giorgio," she said, "you sound upset, this should make you feel a little better."

"Signora, I need more than this," he said, pointing to the tray, "to make me feel better." His face was ashen, and he looked stricken. "Give me a gun," he implored. "That's what I need, to shoot myself."

"Money can be replaced," Rosalia said. "No one has died. Yet."

"My marriage has died," he said. "My wife betrayed me."

Caroline took a sip of orange juice. "I almost died," she said. "I just came out of the hospital, again. I am lucky to be alive."

"Why in the world would anyone want to kill you?" Giorgio asked. He ran his fingers through his hair. He looked irritated.

"It's a long story," she said. "In a nutshell, I told you that my stepdaughter wants to get rid of me."

"A nutshell?"

"Never mind. It's complicated."

Rosalia stepped behind her niece and rubbed her shoulders. "Caroline has had a terrible time."

"Are you sure you are not imagining this?" Giorgio looked Caroline in the eyes. "Overreacting?"

"What a terrible thing to say," said Rosalia with indignation. "What do you know about what my niece has been going through?"

"Women are *regine del drama,* drama queens," he said, softly.

"Excuse me?" Caroline said, "did you just call me a drama queen?"

"Yes. You and all women make a mountain of a hilltop. You, my wife, my ex-wife, my ex-girlfriend, my girlfriend…"

"It's a molehill. It's time you improved your English."

"It's time you improved your Italian," he said, mimicking her voice.

Why don't you just shut up and leave," Caroline said. "Don't expect another euro from me!"

Giorgio stood up and threw his glass on the marble floor. It exploded into a million pieces.

As he walked out and slammed the door, Caroline shouted, "I am removing myself from your bullshit business. It's going to flop big time because you are a loser and losers never win!"

Chapter Forty-Six

The Money Plan

Julia was very resourceful when backed in a corner. They needed money urgently to pay Pia. The woman had kept up her part of the bargain. She had had sex with James and was pregnant.

"Tell me the honest truth," she said to James.

"Here we go again," said James scrolling on his phone. "I've told you a hundred times. I did not enjoy it. Not one bit."

"Well, let's face it, when you came, you had to feel something?"

James looked up from his phone. "Babe, you have to stop. You are driving yourself and me crazy. I felt nothing. Zip. Zero. All I cared about was that my sperm would do its job, and that we would have a baby." He moved closer to her on the bed and put his arm around his wife's shoulders. "We achieved what we had prayed for, a miracle. Pia fell pregnant on the third try. You should be so happy."

"I know. I am happy. Very." Julia looked up at James and smiled wanly. "I am just feeling a bit insecure. It's weird that another woman is carrying our baby. It's your sperm and her egg. She gets to feel the baby move. I feel left out."

"I understand how you feel. We gave this a lot of thought but don't forget that you didn't want to be pregnant, and this was the best solution to having a baby."

"You are right," said Julia. "The only challenge now is how to get the money that we promised Pia."

Julia was in the shower when it finally dawned on her. She grabbed a towel, wrapped it around her body and ran out the bathroom. "James! I have an idea!" she called. She left puddles of water on the tiled floor as she ran barefoot to find her husband. James looked up from his computer.

"I know who will give us the money for Pia," she said breathlessly. "Jill."

Jill, her biological mother, had remarried. Not to the tennis coach, whom she had left her husband for many years ago. That didn't last long. She had married a successful retired entrepreneur, much older than her and despite his health issues, they lived a content life. Over the years, she had kept up sporadic contact with her daughter. Julia made the effort to keep in contact with her mother.

When Julia called her mother, she answered the phone immediately.

Julia first filled her mother in with small talk. She told her that she was in Italy. She spoke about the places she had been to and the people she had met. She could tell that her mother wasn't listening, but she acknowledged the conversation with the correct prompts.

"The only thing that I really want in my life is a baby," Julia said.

"Uh hu…"

"A baby would complete my life. James has longed for a child since we were married. We tried and tried, and it didn't happen."

"Children aren't all they're cracked up to be," said her mother. She yawned. "Believe me, I know."

"Something miraculous and exciting has happened," Julia said. "A friend of ours is carrying our baby for us. She lives in Italy, and she is going to have the baby in Florida."

"This woman is pregnant with your child. How did that happen?"

"I can't get into the logistics," Julia said, "but we are more than thrilled."

"You called to tell me that I am going to be a grandmother?"

"Yes. Isn't that wonderful news?"

"Darling, I wasn't a great mother. What makes you think I will be a doting grandmother? I'm happy for you but don't count on me to take an active part."

"I understand." Julia took a deep breath and her voice shook. "Basically, I need money."

Julia could hear Jill whisper to her husband, "Yup. You were right."

"We have to pay this woman for the inconvenience and the cost of carrying the baby, as well as her flights to the States and her medical costs."

"So, you want me to pay? Is that all this call is about?"

"We are desperate. We don't have the money."

"Why don't you ask your stepmother. She has more money than God."

"I did. She said No. I don't have a good relationship with her."

"That bitch won't give you the money. I heard that she was left a fortune. How much money are you talking about?"

"Only one hundred thousand dollars."

There was silence. Then she said, "You have to be kidding. I don't have that kind of money to give you."

"Think about it this way, Jill." Julia's voice was choked. She continued with a tinge of bitterness. "You have never been there for me. You ran away and left me. You have never given me a cent in all these years." She trembled as she said, "I have never asked you for anything. I am begging you now, because I don't have an alternative."

"Julia, you have to understand. I have had a terrible life. I have suffered and everyone has treated me badly. Except for Bob. There is no way I can give you the money."

Julia started howling. "You have ruined my life in so many ways," she cried. "I have never gotten over the way that you abandoned me."

There was dead silence on the phone. Julia knew that her mother had ended the call. She flung herself at James. "She said no."

They sat in the hotel room, in the dark, not talking. James didn't have any words to console his wife. Julia's phone rang.

"Yes, Jill?" she said.

"I will give you the fucking money!" her mother said, "thanks to my husband. But don't ever ask me for anything again."

"Thank you," Julia whispered.

"Another thing. Don't ever say I am a bad mother. I am better than that bitch Caroline who has stolen your inheritance. I came through for you."

Julia clenched her fist and pulled her arm down. "Yes!" She gesticulated to James. "She said yes."

Chapter Forty-Seven

A Swimming Pool

Salvatore's pride and joy was not his orchard of flourishing fruit trees, or his abundant vegetable garden, it was the swimming pool. He had built it from scratch, by hand, along with a helper named Davide. The rectangle pool, glistening with clear blue water, was a labor of love. He built it for his wife Rosalia, who once told him that one of her greatest pleasures was floating in a swimming pool. Salvatore was a man of action; he immediately took the initiative to make one of his wife's dreams come true. He researched everything about how to build a pool. His friends recommended that he use a reliable pool company; it was far too complicated to build it by himself. But Salvatore enjoyed the challenge. It wasn't the money he told them; it was the satisfaction of achieving a goal, this time—to build a swimming pool.

He sat at his computer and researched how to build a pool. He watched tutorials on YouTube. Salvatore was not unrealistic; he knew that he would need some help. He engaged a young fellow, Davide, who had helped Salvatore with many household projects in the past. Davide left high school early. He was not intellectually gifted, but he was street smart and had gained the respect of his peers.

Growing up, he was teased for his speech impediment and his limp but later he proved himself to be an accomplished artisan. His specialty was building fountains. He used concrete as his medium and created fountains using mythical creatures, Pegasi, angels, and cherubs, spewing water from their mouths. His artistic creations were so admired that many homes in Oristano boasted a *Davide Orso* fountain somewhere in their yard. Although he did not need the extra work, Davide always obliged to help Salvatore. When no one would give him a chance, it was Salvatore who engaged him with projects and paid him well. Davide never forgot that.

Rosalia was quite pleased with the thought of having a pool in their garden but after she saw the mess that it entailed, she wasn't so sure. There were mounds of black soil all over the back yard, and a deep rectangle gaped ominously. Concrete was sprayed all around the pit, and her husband and his assistant left dirty gray footsteps from their work boots all over the patio and the kitchen floor. Rosalia was not happy.

"I am doing this for you, amore," Salvatore told her. "Once the pool is ready and filled you will forget about the mess."

He was right. When the pool was finally finished and the water added, she felt the excitement of a young child who couldn't wait to jump in. At the far end of the pool was a magnificent fountain with dolphins cavorting in a circle. On the very hot days of summer, she and Salvatore would swim in the early mornings before it got too hot, and in the evenings after it cooled down. They even took a dip when the weather was cooler, the pool added joy to their lives.

Rosalia and Caroline sat on the patio overlooking the pool. The blue and white canopy threw shade on their tanned bodies. They had both had a dip in the pool and their wet hair pushed back from their foreheads.

Caroline drank her Aperol Spritz. "I could get used to this," she said.

"My home is your home," Rosalia said. "I mean that. You are welcome here anytime you want."

"Thank you so much, I appreciate that," Caroline said. She stood up and pulled her lounge chair out of the shade. "The truth is after my mother passes; I don't think that I will come back so often."

"You will still have me and Ornella here," Rosalia said. "Don't forget that."

"That's true. I will go and visit my mother one more time before I leave," Caroline said. "It makes me sad because I never know if it will be the last time that I see her. She is not doing well." She rubbed sunscreen over her arms and legs. "I have to be careful, I'm so fair that I burn easily."

"Let me do your back," said Rosalia. "You really are so fair. We are all dark, well, except for Ornella."

"My mother keeps mixing me up with Ornella," Caroline said. "She calls me Ornella all the time."

Rosalia finished spreading the lotion with long strokes all over Caroline's back. She replaced the cap on the tube. "You haven't seen a lot of Ornella since you have been here. Let's call her and make a time to visit her."

"She's been going through so much with Beppe that I didn't want to add to her burden," Caroline said.

"That crisis seems to have been settled for now. They are back together like nothing ever happened," said Rosalia. "Let me call her and ask her when we can come over. When are you leaving the island?"

"In five days" Caroline said. "I'm waiting to hear when Julia and James are leaving. I don't want to leave at the same time. You do know what's going to happen when they arrive in Miami?

"What do you mean? What is going to happen?"

"Julia is going to be arrested. The USA police will be waiting for her."

"Dio mio," Rosalia gasped. "She is getting what she deserves. But it's still shocking."

"This is top secret," Caroline said. She ran her fingers along her lips. "Make sure your lips are zipped," she said. "No one can know."

Rosalia wrapped a towel around herself. Her fingers trembled as she dialed her sister's number. "Ornella?" she said. "Are you free tomorrow afternoon? Caroline and I would like to come over and visit. You are? Good. We need to talk about important things—the very important thing." She clicked the off button.

"What important things?" Caroline asked.

"The things you told me. About Julia."

"No. You can't tell anyone about the upcoming arrest. I told you. This is strictly confidential, no one can know. We don't want Julia to be alerted," Caroline said.

"You are right," said Rosalia. "So we will talk about other things. You know your Aunt Ornella is never short of having interesting things to talk about."

"That's for sure." Caroline laughed.

Chapter Forty-Eight

They Will Know

Salvatore pulled up in front of the wrought iron gates of Beppe and Ornella's seaside villa. Rosalia and Caroline stepped out of the car.

"I will be down at the pier meeting up with my buddies," Salvatore said. "Text me when you are ready to go home."

Rosalia nodded. She was wearing a green pantsuit and her white loafers that she kept for special occasions. Rosalia always sought her older sister's approval on the way she dressed. Caroline, on the other hand, had a knack for always putting the right clothes with the right accessories together. She knew exactly how to knot a scarf in the perfect way. Her kitten heeled pumps, together with a cream linen sleeveless dress, were perfect for lunch on the patio overlooking the sea.

Signor and Signora Accadi's villa in Torre Grande was opulent yet welcoming. Cerise colored bougainvillea trailed down the white plaster walls which always make the exterior of a home look appealing, particularly with a blue sky and a matching ocean as the backdrop.

The housemaid, Elena, let them in. Rosalia had known her since she was a young girl who came from the village to work for the Accadis. When Beppe and Ornella separated briefly, it was Elena who took the situation very badly. She ended up in the hospital on an IV for shock.

"My darlings!" Ornella, wearing a Pucci caftan, called out. She descended the circular staircase like a movie star from the 1960s. Following her were their two Yorkies, Remy and Lily. She hugged her sister and her niece. "These two doggies"—she said, pointing to them—"are the reason why Beppe and I are together."

Caroline wasn't sure if she should laugh. It sounded silly but it was true. Beppe had come back home from his mistress for the sole reason that he missed his dogs.

They sat on floral linen sofas opposite each other.

"How are things with you and Beppe?" Rosalia asked.

"To be honest, Beppe is here in person but not in mind," said Ornella.

Rosalia took a handful of nuts and cupped them in her mouth. "What do you mean?" she asked, with her mouth full.

"I wouldn't say this to anyone else." She turned to see if Elena was out of earshot. "But Beppe is not a happy man."

"Are you saying he regrets coming back?"

"For sure he regrets being with me. He created this mess, so he has to live with it. Not my problem."

Rosalia's brows furrowed, and she brushed imaginary crumbs off her lap. "Beppe didn't think things through. He moved in with that other woman too fast. He made a big mistake, and I think he regrets it."

"Well, he was punished by his stupid choices. The biggest punishment is that I made him sell the yacht."

"You did?" Rosalia asked, shocked. "You loved that boat, and it was named after you."

Ornella sighed. "I didn't love it that much anymore when I found out that he used to meet up with her on the boat, in our cabin."

"*Che scandalo!* What a scandal!" Rosalia said.

Ornella turned to Caroline, "I believe you've been through a terrible time. How are you doing now?"

"I'm still alive," Caroline said, "so I guess I'm doing well. It's better than the alternative."

"What alternative?" said Rosalia.

"Being dead."

"What a crazy thing," Ornella said. "Who would have thought that your own stepdaughter would be so evil. It sounds like *Rigoletta*, Verdi's opera." She called out to Elena to bring three glasses of lemonade. "I made it myself this morning," she said. "We Bellini women are resilient. You will get through this and triumph." She squeezed Caroline's hand.

Rosalia rubbed her chin and closed her eyes like she just had remembered something. She turned to Caroline. "What is happening with your skincare business with

Giorgio Lanconi from Bosa? How is it going to work with you leaving back to America?"

Caroline pursed his lips. "That is not happening anymore," she said. "You were all right about him. He wasn't interested in me or opening a business. His plan was to scam me and take all my money."

"I tried to warn you," said Rosalia. "Did he get your money?"

"I'm smarter than that. Giorgio underestimated me. He thought he could charm an older, American woman and fleece her. It's such a cliché."

Elena brought in the tray of glasses with lemonade and a sprig of mint. She put them on the center coffee table. The three women stopped talking while she was in the room. They waited for her to leave.

"I played my cards right," Caroline continued. "He asked me to put money in his account."

"You didn't, right?" Ornella said.

"I did."

"You did?" they both cried out.

"Shh…" Caroline hissed. "This is confidential." She lowered her voice to a whisper and moved closer to them. "I had the opportunity twice to get all his personal information and login details of his bank account. The first time I saw his bank statements lying on his desk, I quickly took a screenshot on my phone. The second time he gave me all his banking information where I was supposed to deposit my money. I pretended that I was speaking to my financial advisor, and he fell for it."

"Wow," Ornella said.

"You are so smart," Rosalia added.

"Here comes the best part. I emptied out his account. All the money I had deposited and then all of his as well." Caroline couldn't stop herself from laughing.

"Has he discovered this yet?" said Rosalia. Her eyes wide in awe.

"The idiot came screaming at me, but he thinks that his wife took it all. Because guess what? She has disappeared. When I heard that I thought how lucky am I?"

"The family was concerned that you had fallen for Giorgio's charm and were going to do something stupid," said Rosalia.

"You shouldn't have underestimated me," said Caroline. "I played him from the beginning."

Rosalia looked at her watch. "The time has flown. I must text Salvatore to come and get us.

Ornella walked them to the door. She stopped just before turning the handle. She put her arm around Caroline. "There is something I need to tell you before you leave Sardinia," she said. Ornella's expression turned very serious.

Caroline stopped and turned towards her aunt. "What is it?" She could sense that her aunt was nervous. "You can tell me anything."

"I am not your aunt," Ornella said. Her lower lip quivered.

"Then who are you?" asked Caroline.

"I am your *real* mother."

Chapter Forty-Nine

What is a Mother?

"What? What did you just say?" asked Caroline. She held onto the doorframe to stop herself from falling down.

Rosalia put her arm around Caroline's waist and ushered her back inside. Caroline looked dazed. "Sit down, sit down," said Rosalia, pushing Caroline towards a chair.

Ornella spoke. "I've wanted to tell you for a very long time. The time was never right but I can't keep it a secret anymore." Ornella closed her eyes and took a deep breath. "I am your mother," she said.

Caroline's eyes darted between her two aunts. "What does she mean?" she asked Rosalia.

"You kept telling me that your mother keeps repeating Ornella's name to you," said Rosalia. "I think it's because she is trying to tell you something. I told Ornella about this, and we both decided that it's time to tell you the truth." Rosalia glanced at her sister. "Ornella you tell her."

Ornella bowed her head. She was silent while trying to come up with the right words. She looked up and studied Caroline's face before she told her the truth. "When I was sixteen, I fell pregnant out of wedlock. I had a boyfriend of the same age. We both went to the same school. It took me some time to build up the courage to tell my parents. In those days a pregnancy out of wedlock was a travesty that brought shame to the family. My parents were very angry. I could bear their anger, but it was their disappointment in me that hurt the most. Abortion was not a consideration; it was illegal. I was sent away to my mother's cousin in Naples. No one knew, not even the boy." Ornella blew her nose. Her hands shook as she took a sip of water. "After you were born, my parents came up with a plan. Your mother, Claudia, was married and they were having trouble conceiving. I was forced to give you up as a newborn to Claudia. We were sworn to secrecy." Then she added, "To this day, Beppe doesn't know this secret."

Caroline was not only stunned but she was angry. "It's a terrible thing you did by not telling me. After all these years."

"Your parents loved you as their own," Rosalia said. "You were the pride and joy of their lives."

Caroline put her head down on the table and didn't move. She felt that the life force of her body had drained away.

"Are you okay?" asked Rosalia.

"No, I am not okay," she said in a muffled voice. "My whole life is a lie." She raised her head and turned to Ornella. "How could you have pretended all these years? Surely each time you looked at me, you must have thought that I am your daughter. Didn't you even care?"

"I cared very much." She wiped her tears away with her hand.

"It's a little too late to start crying now," said Caroline. "I will never look at you as my mother. My mother is the one who raised me and took care of me my whole life. She is the one whom I love. Not you."

Suddenly things started making sense to Caroline. Her parents were not wealthy, but there was always food on the table and a roof over her head. The house that they lived in was down the road from her two aunts. When there were additional expenses, like her baptism, or a dress for a special occasion, she never went without. Caroline went to a private Catholic school and went on all the trips when her class traveled to other towns. She visited the Vatican in Rome with her school and to Switzerland in her final year. She never asked where the money came from, but she knew that the extra gifts came from her aunt Ornella. She was never told to say thank you. Caroline took it for granted. Her aunt and uncle were very wealthy, and she was a part of their lives. Now it started to make sense to her. She didn't feel gratitude, she felt angry.

Salvatore arrived to pick them up and he honked the horn impatiently.

"Don't tell anyone," said Ornella. "It will complicate matters."

"Obviously, it's very easy for you to keep secrets," said Caroline. "Lying must be second nature to you." She looked at Rosalia. "That goes for you too."

"This has weighed heavy on our hearts," said Rosalia, "but we knew that you were happy and when you left for America with your parents, it didn't make sense for us to disrupt your life."

"Now I know, where I got my blonde hair and blue eyes from," said Caroline. "That should have been a sign." She stood up and looked out the window. She waved to Salvatore and mouthed that they were coming down. "My mother was trying to tell me something. Either she thought I was you, because we look similar, or she was trying to tell me that you were my mother, not her. I hope it's the first, because she is my true mother, and I would be sad to think that she didn't think so."

"I hope you will find it in your heart to forgive me," said Ornella. "Things were very different in those days. Being an unwed mother had stigma. It brought shame to the whole family. I felt lucky that my beautiful baby girl was going to my sister whom I loved. That was so much better than her growing up in an orphanage or being adopted by another family. I knew that you were well taken care of and loved. The most important part to me was that I got to see you grow up. That brought me peace."

Rosalia put her arms around Caroline. "I know you feel betrayed. This is a lot for you to take in. Ornella and I wanted to tell you many times, but the circumstances weren't right. When your mother no longer had a memory, we thought it was the time to tell you the truth. Claudia and your father were wonderful parents. You were raised with so much love. That made it easier for us."

Salvatore honked and shouted out the car window. "What's taking you so long? You women can't say goodbye in a timely manner. Come on, before the traffic gets bad."

Rosalia kissed Ornella on her cheek and when Ornella offered her cheek to Caroline, she recoiled and walked down the steps towards the car. Everything seemed familiar yet everything had changed. The one thing that Caroline wanted to do most of all was visit her mother and give her a big hug and a kiss. In her heart she knew that Claudia was her real mother.

Chapter Fifty

The Confession

Caroline pulled up a chair and reached for her mother's hand. It was small, childlike and surprisingly wrinkle-free. She stroked the soft skin with her thumb.

"You will always be my mama," said Caroline, "no matter what."

Her mother looked up without blinking. She peered at her daughter, confused, as if trying to remember who she was.

A nurse put her head around the door. "Can I bring you anything?" she asked.

Caroline shook her head.

"If you need anything just press the bell," she said, and left.

Caroline's body felt heavy. Her head felt as if it was about to explode. She was leaving Sardinia in the next few days, and she wanted to tell her mother many things. She hoped that it would give her some relief.

"I'm a good person, Mama," she said, clearing her throat. "I have done things that maybe not be right, but I had no choice. Do you remember our cat, Domingo? He once hid under my bed and when I tried to pull him out, he bit me on my face. I ran to you crying with blood dripping down. You told me that it wasn't his fault. You explained that he was trapped and afraid, so he lashed out. You said that I must forgive him."

Caroline bit her lower lip. She let go of her mother's hand, stood up and quietly shut the door. She pulled up the multi-colored crocheted blanket over her mother's lap.

"Just like Domingo under the bed, I have been trapped and afraid. I have done things that I am not proud of, but I did them only to survive. I have told you that Julia has tried to harm me, and I do believe that she wants me dead. I am a smart woman, and I had to come up with a plan. Mama, I have lied to everyone including the police. It was *me* who set up the scenarios to incriminate Julia. She is evil and I needed to prove that."

Her mother didn't flinch. She didn't register what Caroline was saying.

"I concocted the three phony attempts by Julia on my life. The first was my near drowning on the yacht. That one just happened without a plan. I was tired from snorkeling, and I had difficulty getting back on the boat. Julia held out her hand for me to grab. I purposely let it go. This was a perfect opportunity to blame her. It worked.

"The second plot, I put a lot of thought into. We were in the Costa Smeralda at a hotel. After we came back from dinner, I pretended to pass out. I planted an anti-freeze container in Julia's make-up bag. I made sure to take photos." Caroline smiled. "Cell phones are very convenient to take screen shots. Technology really has come a long way. DNA has made big advances too. I placed a tissue with Julia's DNA on the lid of the container."

Caroline stood up and put her ear to the closed door, it was quiet. "Where was I? Oh. I wanted to show that someone had a malicious intent towards me. I dug up Chicco the cat from his grave and placed the dirty, foul-smelling carcass on my bed." Caroline wrinkled her nose. "It was so vile that I nearly threw up. Of course I wore gloves." She chuckled. "Like a Mafia movie."

The old lady sneezed, and snot came flying out her nose. Caroline jumped up, got a tissue and wiped her mother's nose lovingly. "Are you proud of me, Mama?" she asked. "I always wanted you to be proud of me. You taught me to stand up for myself."

Caroline's phone buzzed. It was Rosalia. "Hello. I am visiting my mother," she said. "I'm okay. I'm very disturbed about the revelation that Ornella is my birth mother, but you know what? My mother is my mother. There is no doubt about that." She ended the call.

Caroline rubbed her hands together and continued. "The third staged attempt on my life was when we all went out for dinner to Mama Sofia's. By the way I know that Ornella is my biological mother, but *you* are my forever mother, so don't worry about that. There, Ornella had a meltdown and tried to stab Laura, Beppe's mistress. You know what a philanderer he is. Julia had to get involved, she grabbed the knife away from Ornella and guess what? I saw an opportunity—I jumped in front of the knife, and she stabbed me in the arm."

There was a tap at the door. "*Buon Giorno*, Good Afternoon." The lunch lady walked in with a tray. "Do you need me to help or are you going to feed your mother?" she asked.

"I will feed her. Thank you," said Caroline. The lady left. Caroline cut up the chicken into small pieces. She wheeled the table in front of her mother's wheelchair and placed the tray on it. She held a cup of water for her mother to sip through a straw. Caroline then held a spoonful of rice and gravy up to her mother's lips. Her mother turned her head.

"Open up," Caroline coaxed.

Her mother pursed her lips. Caroline tried with a piece of chicken. "It's yummy, you love chicken. Open your mouth, please."

Her mother pursed her lips even harder. She swatted Caroline's hand away.

"I can see that you don't want to eat," Caroline said. She wiped her mother's mouth. "We will try again in a little bit."

Caroline found that telling her mother the truth, even if she didn't understand, was very cathartic. A heavy burden was lifted off her shoulders.

"The fourth incident I want to tell you about I orchestrated very carefully. I thought of every detail. I gathered all the evidence so that I could present my case to the authorities that would show without a doubt that Julia wanted to get rid of me. I have filed a case with the police and guess what? She is going to be arrested as soon as she puts a foot on American soil."

Her mother yawned.

Caroline smiled to herself and, if she could have, she would have patted herself on the back for the good work that she had done.

"James was in Oristano this entire time, staying in a hotel. I went there to confront them. They were plotting their own scheme. Believe me, Mama, you don't know them, they are bad apples. When I was leaving, the elevator was not functioning properly. It stopped between floors and would not budge. I could tell that the jump down into the carriage was only a few feet. If it had been farther, a fall could end in death. I knew that was not the case. I jumped and I screamed, "Why Julia, why?" That was recorded on the security camera. I always wanted to take acting lessons, and you wouldn't let me, but I am a natural actress."

The old lady closed her eyes, and she snored lightly.

"You must be thinking why would I go to all these lengths to incriminate this girl? Because she has a motive to get rid of me. Julia is waiting for me to go, *bye-bye,* so that she gets the money. My husband, may he rest in peace, put a no contest clause in the will *that specifies that anyone who challenges the will or interferes with the provisions forfeits their inheritance*." Caroline burst out laughing, "No one is ever going to know it's me and not that spoiled brat."

Her mother mumbled in her sleep. The mumbling grew louder, and soon she was screaming. Piercing sounds of pain and anger.

Caroline rushed out of the door. "Please come quickly, my mother is in pain."

A nurse came back with Caroline to the room. "What is the matter?" she asked in a soothing voice. "Did anything upset her?" the nurse asked Caroline.

"Nothing that I can think of," she said.

Her mother became very agitated and soon calmed down after the nurse injected her.

"I have to get going," said Caroline.

She kissed her mother on the cheek and left the room.

Caroline nodded to the lady at the reception desk and waved goodbye. She took a deep breath. There was a spring in her step. After confessing to her mother, Caroline felt much lighter. She passed a busker playing his guitar and singing. Caroline threw some euros in the upturned hat and broke into a jig. She knew that Julia and James were leaving the next morning and when they landed in Miami, they were in for a big surprise. Caroline tried not to laugh when she pictured Julia's shock when she was led away in handcuffs.

Chapter Fifty-One

Secrets and Lies

Ernesto Gambino, chief of police put down the phone and let out a long whistle. He ran his hands over his hair. Chief Gambino did that when he felt overwhelmed. The sensation of his fingers skimming over his buzz cut calmed him down.

"Please get hold of Signor Salvatore Rossi," he called out to his secretary. He picked up the phone as soon as it buzzed.

"Salvo," he said, "where are you?"

"Is something the matter?" Salvatore answered. It wasn't usual that the chief called him out of the blue, by his nickname.

"I have a very unexpected development about the case of the attempted murder suspect Julia Callahan to share with you."

"My wife and I are having lunch at Mama Sofia's. Can you meet us here?" Salvatore asked. He mouthed to Rosalia, "Gambino has some news."

"Please wait for me, I shouldn't be long," he said. "Order the *Ossobuco* for me."

Rosalia put a forkful of her chicken piccata in her mouth. "I wonder what he wants to tell you?" she said, with a mouth full.

"Tell *us*, he said. "This is your family."

"True." Rosalia sipped her wine. She looked at Salvatore and asked, "Is my family causing you too much stress?"

Salvatore leaned over and squeezed his wife's hand. "When I married you, I married the whole package." He beamed. "My life used to be pretty boring."

"You mean *peaceful*," she said. Rosalia lifted his hand and kissed it. "I really appreciate all that you do for me."

"Two lovebirds," said Mama Sophia, refilling their water glasses. "It makes my heart happy to see." She sighed. "I have not been so lucky in my life."

Salvatore changed the subject. "Can I please place an order of your ossobuco? It's for Chief Gambino. He will be joining us."

"Of course," she said. "I will bring it out when he arrives. "Chief Gambino does not like his food cold."

Moments later, Chief Gambino strode in like he owned the place. He wore his coat over his shoulders like a sail on a ship. The diners looked up. Some greeted him, while others turned their heads. It depended on which side of the law they were on. He was the kind of man that made one feel guilty even when you were not. When his police car drove behind another vehicle, one made sure to drive at the exact speed posted and to make a full stop at each light. Chief Gambino was a powerful man in town.

He threw his hat on the hat stand and gave his coat to the hostess at her station. He spotted Salvatore and Rosalia right away and made his way to the table. He shook each of their hands and even though he was on duty he still asked for the house wine.

He rubbed his hands together. "I can smell the ossobuco," he said and on cue Mama Sophia placed his dish in front of him. It was piping hot. He took a slice of sourdough bread and tore off a piece. He dipped it in olive oil, swirled it around and popped it in his mouth. He took a swig of wine before he cut into the veal. The Chief grumbled under his breath, "The meat is tough." He put down his knife and fork and said firmly but softly, "*Signora e signore*. Lady and gentleman, I have news of an interesting turn of events to tell you."

Salvatore and Rosalia pushed their chairs closer and leaned in.

"This morning, the head of security at the *Sacro Cuore Degli Angeli*, the assisted living facility, where your sister Signora Claudia Bellini resides, called me with very disturbing news. The facility recently put in cameras and sound recording devices because they were experiencing a slew of thefts from the residents' rooms."

"What did they find? Was my sister being abused by the staff?" said Rosalia.

"No. But this development is equally troubling. They have a recording of your niece, Caroline Anderson, in conversation with her mother. It is very clear, concise and damning."

"What did she say? Is it bad?"

"It's worse than bad, it's terrible —for your niece. On the surveillance audio, she confesses to her mother that she orchestrated the murder plots, not Julia. She wanted to frame her. Caroline went into great detail about how she set this all up."

Rosalia's eyes widened. She clapped her hand over her mouth.

"This is insane," said Salvatore. "Are you saying that she made all those stories up?"

"Yes."

"Everything was a lie?" said Rosalia.

"Yes."

"Why would Caroline do such a thing? Does she hate her stepdaughter that much?"

"Yes."

"The anti-freeze, the knife attack, the elevator fall? They didn't happen like that?" Rosalia said.

"Correct. She set everything up herself to look like those things happened to her. And she framed her stepdaughter."

"That's so devious," Rosalia said. "I can't believe it."

"You better believe it," Chief Gambino answered. "Everything is there on the recording. Everything."

"What will happen now?" Salvatore said. "Julia and her husband are on their way back home."

"I contacted the authorities in Miami, to suspend the arrest due to new information about the case."

"How will Caroline be punished for this?"

Ernesto Gambino took a sip of wine and wiped his mouth on a napkin. He then proceeded to cover his mouth with one hand while he picked his teeth with a toothpick with the other. Salvatore and Rosalia waited for him to finish.

He cleared his throat. "Unfortunately, your niece cannot be arrested for lying and concocting a story, because no one was hurt, excepting her. The young lady to whom this happened, Julia, will have to sue her stepmother in court in Italy for false reporting and defamation of character. There is also the fraudulent act of staging a crime. It is up to her if she wants to take this further."

"This is too terrible," said Rosalia. "I could never imagine that Caroline could be so deceitful. I have known her since she was born and nothing in her character ever showed that."

"Signora, greed can do that to people. I have seen it all. Nothing shocks me. In this situation Caroline knew that her husband included a "no contest clause' in his will. It states that if anyone challenges or contests his will, they will forfeit their distribution. Do you understand?"

"Does that mean that if Caroline could prove Julia was trying to kill her, she would lose everything her father was going to give her?" said Rosalia.

'Precisely," Chief Gambino said. "There is one thing I would like you both to do for me."

"Of course," Salvatore and Rosalia agreed in unison.

"Please do not say one word about this to Caroline. Or anyone. This is highly confidential and if you do, it would be deemed as an obstruction of justice. Do I have your word?"

"Yes," they both answered.

Chief Gambino put on his hat, threw his coat over his shoulders and with a quick goodbye, he walked out the door.

Chapter Fifty-Two

The Game is Up

The suitcase lay open on the bed. Caroline laid all her clothes, shoes and bags beside it. She was an experienced traveler and an expert packer. Instead of placing her garments flat, she rolled each item so that they fit snugly like dachshund puppies taking an afternoon nap. Caroline was getting ready to leave that evening and would be back in Miami the following morning.

Rosalia knocked lightly on the door. "How is the packing going?" she asked.

"I'm now sorry that I was tempted to buy so many things. I'm having trouble fitting everything in." She avoided eye contact.

"It looks like you are managing very well," said Rosalia. "Are you looking forward to going home?"

"I'm not happy to be leaving all of you but I can't wait to get away from all this drama."

Adela poked her head through the door, "I just received a text from Julia. They arrived safe and sound."

"Are they back home?" Rosalia asked.

"Yes. She, James and Pia. They had a good flight."

Caroline felt the room spin and she sat down on the bed. She felt faint and put her head between her legs. She was not aware that the charges against Julia had been dropped and therefore she was not apprehended on her arrival in Miami.

"Are you okay?" asked Adela.

She didn't answer.

Rosalia brought her a glass of water. "Are you not feeling well?" she asked.

Caroline took a shaky breath and nodded slowly. "I'm fine," she said. She pushed the glass of water away. "I've had a rough few days," she said. "It's all finally getting to me."

She had to call Chief Gambino. He had told her that Julia would be apprehended as soon as she stepped on to US soil. Why had that not happened? She also understood that it wasn't her place to question the chief of police. There had to be an explanation.

Caroline checked her watch. She knew that there was something she had to do before leaving Sardinia. She made an excuse to Rosalia and left the house. She knew the fastest route to the police headquarters in Cagliari was just over an hour by train. It was still early in the day, and she figured she could get there and back in time for her flight. First, she called the precinct without giving her name, to make sure that the Chief was there; he was.

Caroline arrived at the police headquarters in record time. She walked in as if she owned the place. She had learned a long time ago that if you looked as though you belonged, no one would question you.

"Buongiorno," she said to the officer through a glass partition. "I'm here to see Chief Gambino."

"Is he expecting you?"

"Yes. Please tell him Signora Caroline Anderson is here to see him."

Caroline paced the floor and waited. It seemed to take forever. She wrung her hands and bit her lip. Unknown to her, the security camera filmed her: she was the image of a woman in distress. A connecting door opened, and a young woman appeared. She asked Caroline to follow her. The woman punched in some numbers and the door swung open. They walked down a bland corridor with bright fluorescent lighting. Chief Gambino stood at the opening of his office, smoking.

"What brings you here?" he asked, annoyed. "Don't you have a flight tonight?"

"Yes, I do. I need to speak to you urgently."

"What is it?" he asked. He walked through the door and sat at his desk. Caroline followed him.

"Why wasn't Julia arrested at the airport in Miami?" she blurted out.

"What business is that of yours?" He put on his glasses and peered at the computer screen.

"I just heard from my family that Julia, her husband, and the surrogate, arrived at the home last night without a hitch." She looked at him accusingly. "That's not what you told me was going to happen."

Chief Gambino rubbed his jaw as if debating whether to tell her. "I will be brief, Signora." A crease formed between his brows. "There was a change of plan. We, meaning our investigators, discovered that your stepdaughter was not the culprit of these terrible crimes."

"What do you mean?" Caroline said. She stumbled and sat down. "Then who is?"

"To put it bluntly. It was you."

"Is this a joke?"

Chief Gambino shook his head. He spoke as if he was reprimanding a child. "Your game is up, Signora. We know exactly how and what you did."

Caroline was stone-faced. Her right eye developed a tic. "I think I know what is happening here," she said. "Has somebody paid you to change the whole story and blame me?" She looked affronted. "I heard about these things that happen here."

"You should be very careful what you say," the Chief said. "You are making false accusations about our justice system. But before you continue, you are already in big trouble. We have all the evidence we need to prove that you set this all up in order to trap your stepdaughter."

"Oh please," Caroline said, indignantly. Her left eye began to tic also.

"When you last visited your mother at the assisted living facility, everything that you said was recorded. They had installed a sophisticated camera and audio system. You thought you were so clever, but you didn't think this through."

Caroline went pale. She sat slumped in the chair and couldn't find the right words to say. "Does this mean that I am going to be arrested?" she said in a monotone.

"In this country." Chief Gambino held up his fingers to count the offenses. "You can be accused of false reporting, defamation of character, obstruction of justice, and staging a crime. It is up to your stepdaughter to lay charges." He called for a cup of coffee and did not offer Caroline any. Chief Gambino stood up, rubbed his hands together to let Caroline know that there was nothing else to discuss. He showed her the door. "You can leave tonight," he said. "The consequences of your devious actions have been recorded, noted, and forwarded to the authorities in your country. What they want to do with it is up to them. The only thing that saddens me is that your dear Aunt Rosalia doesn't deserve a niece like you. Your mother is fortunate that she doesn't know what a disappointment her daughter is."

Chapter Fifty-Three

Home is Where the Heart is

"Yes, please I'd love some champagne," Caroline said. The flight attendant smiled and placed a champagne glass on Caroline's table. They had just reached cruising height and Caroline unclicked her seatbelt. She felt happy, almost exhilarated, to be flying home to Miami. A handsome, gray-haired gentleman sat alongside her. She turned to greet him, but he did not look her way.

Caroline preferred her privacy, but she thought it would be rude to pull up the partition between them so soon into the flight. She would do that when dinner was served.

When he stood up to remove his laptop from the overhead compartment, Caroline noted how elegantly he was dressed. He wore a pale-yellow cashmere sweater pulled over neatly pressed khaki slacks. Round tortoiseshell glasses added to his intellectual air, and his gold watch was classy but understated. When he was seated, Caroline checked for a wedding ring, there wasn't one.

"Are you visiting Miami or on your way back home?" she asked him.

"I'm going back home," he said. He adjusted his sweater, pulling it over his round belly.

"Me too," she said, flashing him a smile. "I spent some time in Sardinia, my favorite place in the whole world, but I'm happy to be going home."

He nodded, opened his laptop, and focused on the screen. Caroline pegged her seat mate as either a CEO of a large company or an attorney. Stuart too had dressed elegantly but not in a flashy way. He had never wanted his clients to think that he was making too much money off of them.

While Caroline sipped her champagne, her seatmate drank water out of a bottle. He cupped his warmed peanuts in the palm of his hand, shaking them before popping them into his mouth.

Caroline cocked her head and flashed him a big smile. "I wonder why we all shake the nuts before we eat them," she said.

He lifted his head and looked at her, confused, as if he wasn't sure that he heard right. "Pardon?" he asked.

"It's just something that I've noticed," she said. "When people take a handful of nuts to eat, they first give them a shake."

"Oh," he said. "I've never noticed that."

She wanted to explain that she enjoyed studying people and found their small idiosyncrasies fascinating. But she didn't. She picked up right away that he wasn't the chatty type.

She lifted the menu from the side pocket of her seat and perused the dinner options. Caroline hadn't realized how hungry she was. She had hardly eaten anything due to the stressful day. The flight attendant greeted her by name and asked for her beverage of choice with her dinner. Caroline opted for a glass of red wine. The seatmate asked for a tomato juice.

"That's another observation of mine," she said to him, "passengers on flights drink tomato juice more than any other time. I wonder why that is?"

He shot her a quizzical look.

"The filet or the sole?" she called out to *Mr. Unfriendly.* "Which do you think is the better choice?"

He lifted his headphones from one ear.

"Meat or the fish? What do you suggest?" Caroline persisted.

"This lady wants to know which dish to choose," he said to the flight attendant hovering near them. "Can you please ask the head chef in the galley for his suggestion and let her know."

The flight attendant laughed. Caroline's face turned red. She was annoyed that he was mocking her. He then asked the flight attendant for caviar and blinis and requested his main course be served in two hours.

Caroline ate her steak in silence. She felt uneasy. Her unfriendly seatmate, although immersed in a movie, lifted his eyes off the screen and occasionally glanced at her. He seemed to be disapproving of the amount of alcohol she was imbibing. *Screw him,* she thought as she lifted the partition and shut him off from her view.

Caroline went to the lavatory and changed into the pajamas that had been placed on her seat. She reclined her seat to the flatbed position and wrapped herself in a soft blanket. It had been a very stressful few weeks in Italy. She was disappointed in herself. Caroline was a plotter and a planner. She prided herself on that. This time she had messed up the details. She had underestimated the security at her mother's assisted living facility. Evidently safety topped privacy in these places, and she had not taken hidden cameras into account.

Caroline was also worried how far Julia and James would take legal action against her. She hoped that now that they were going to be new parents, they wouldn't have the money, time or energy to pursue legal charges against her in a foreign country.

She drifted off to sleep and the next thing she knew, breakfast was about to be served. Caroline awoke to the sounds of clanking in the galley as the crew were preparing the morning meal. She put her seat into the upright position and stood up to go to the lavatory. She peered over the partition and saw that her seatmate was drinking coffee. There was a breakfast tray on his table. She waved to him, but he did not wave back. When she got to the restroom, there was a line of people waiting their turn.

"I can't understand why they have so few toilets," she said to a woman carrying a sleepy toddler. "For the whole of business class, there are only two," she complained.

When it was her turn, Caroline shut the door and locked it. She emptied her bladder trying not to step on the pee on the floor. It was so cramped that she could hardly turn around to look at her reflection in the mirror. She was not a pretty sight. Her hair stood up in the front like a woodpecker and it was flattened in the back. Her face was pale, and her eyes had dark smudges below them. She studied herself. *Do I look innocent or evil?* She settled on tired, and she looked her age. Her skin was translucent, like a flower that had been pressed and dried. She splashed cold water on her face. She zipped open her make-up bag and took out her moisturizer. She patted some over her face. Then she ringed her eyes with a gray pencil and put mascara on her lashes. Her face started coming back to life. She added blusher to her cheeks and nude lip gloss to her lips. She fixed her hair, and she changed back into her clothes. Someone banged on the toilet door. When she emerged, she was surprised to see that it was her seatmate.

"What took you so long?" he asked, annoyed. "We are all waiting to go." He pointed to the line of angry people.

By the time she got back to her seat, her breakfast was on her tray. She had only eaten a few mouthfuls of scrambled egg and a few sips of her watered-down coffee by the time the pilot announced that they were starting the descent.

The flight crew came through the cabin with large plastic bags to collect trash and earphones. All seats were put in an upright position and the partitions between the seats pushed down in preparation for landing. Caroline nodded to her neighbor. He looked back at her with disdain.

The plane landed smoothly. A flight attendant thanked everyone. Caroline collected her belongings.

Then the pilot made an announcement. "Ladies and gentlemen, we ask you to please stay in your seats. We have a sick passenger who needs to deplane first. Thank you for your co-operation."

Caroline looked up and flinched as her unfriendly seatmate stood in front of her. "I don't need your help to take my carry-on down," she said to him, "but thank you."

She felt sorry that she had misjudged him. He wasn't so unfriendly after all. The man bent down and grabbed her arm. He said quietly but firmly, "Please co-operate and stand up."

"What are you doing?" she asked. "Take your hands off of me."

He tightened his grip around her arm and yanked her up out of her seat. She felt that every eye on the plane was turned towards her. The exit door flung open and three armed police officers barged in and surrounded her. Her mouth opened in shock.

"Caroline Anderson," the unfriendly seatmate said, "I am with the FBI. You are under arrest." He flashed his badge at her.

Two police officers grabbed Caroline by the arms and led her off the plane.

"There is a mistake," Caroline said, as she was dragged off. "This is crazy. I can explain everything." Her eyes darted wildly. "I only wanted to teach her a lesson. I never meant to harm her," she whimpered.

As soon as they got to the gate area, the officer put Caroline's hands behind her back and handcuffed her.

"You can't do this!" she cried. "What did I do?"

"You are under arrest for the murder of your husband, Stuart Anderson," the FBI agent with the pale-yellow cashmere sweater said. "Anything that you say or do can be held against you."

All the color drained from Caroline's face. "My husband?" she whispered. "I killed Stuart?"

The unfriendly FBI agent looked her dead in the face and said, "Yes. You killed him."

He lowered her head as she got into the back seat of the police car.

"I killed my husband. You are right," she said. "He was an asshole." She turned to face the agent. "But I want you to know that I'm not a bad person."

About the Author

Bonita Fabian was born in South Africa and spent most of her life traveling and writing stories about her experiences for magazines and newspapers. She lived in Italy for a few years where she fell in love with the people and the culture. After her four children were raised, she realized her lifelong aspiration of becoming an accomplished novelist. She lives with in Miami, Florida.

Also by Bonita Fabian

They Will Know: A Gripping Psychological Thriller With a Shocking Twist

One missing baby. Two shattered families. Too many secrets to count.

A baby girl disappears from her stroller parked outside a restaurant in Denmark while her mother eats lunch inside. Authorities are notified and a massive manhunt is launched. Two thousand miles away in Sardinia, Italy, a young man shows up with a newborn baby. He gives the baby to his wife, who is still grieving the loss of their stillborn child.

A longtime boarder in the family home hears the news about a missing baby in Copenhagen and becomes suspicious when he learns that the young husband had recently returned from there. The boarder grapples with his loyalty and affection for his host family and doing the right thing for this baby. Interpol investigates and the shocking truth about the baby girl's identity is revealed.

Order your copy:
https://www.amazon.com/author/bonniefabian.1-